Capturing the
Texas Rancher's Heart

Capturing the Texas Rancher's Heart

A Tremaynes of Texas Romance

Debra Holt

TULE
PUBLISHING

Capturing the Texas Rancher's Heart
Copyright© 2021 Debra Holt
Tule Publishing First Printing, June 2021

The Tule Publishing, Inc.

ALL RIGHTS RESERVED

First Publication by Tule Publishing 2021

Cover design by Lee Hyat Designs

No part of this book may be used or reproduced in any manner whatsoever without written permission except in the case of brief quotations embodied in critical articles and reviews.

This is a work of fiction. Names, characters, places, and incidents are products of the author's imagination or are used fictitiously. Any resemblance to actual events, locales, organizations, or persons, living or dead, is entirely coincidental.

ISBN: 978-1-953647-65-8

Chapter One

"'S'cuse me." The voice came out of nowhere...hesitant, almost timid, and barely above a squeak. "S'cuse me, please?" It repeated itself with more volume and brought the nurse's head up, eyes searching.

Jamie Westmoreland rose from her chair situated behind the nurse's desk and peered over the edge of the console. She saw a large white straw cowboy hat, red and blue plaid western shirt, huge silver buckle, denim jeans over brown cowboy boots. There was nothing new about seeing males in those parts dressed in such attire. What set this one apart was the fact he was only about three or four feet tall, and the hat appeared to be larger than his whole upper body.

As his head moved backward on his neck to gaze up at her over the tall desk, the too-big, too-loose hat tipped farther back on his head and allowed two bright blue eyes to come into view. They were large and wide-eyed in a face smattered with freckles across the nose and upper cheekbones.

Something in those eyes caught smack in the middle of her chest. Jamie couldn't help the spread of warmth softening the smile that automatically curved the corners of her mouth. She straightened and moved around the desk to stand, hands on hips, looking down at the small figure.

"How can I help you?"

"I'm Thomas Andrew Tremayne, the third one, and I'm six years old. But I'll be seven in a month. I want to see my dad…please."

Her smile broadened. "And who is your dad?"

"His name is Thomas Andrew Tremayne, Junior. The second one. He's a lot older 'n me."

Jamie bit the inside of her lip to maintain professional composure and keep in check the wide grin that threatened to pop out. This little boy was trying to be so matter-of-fact and grown-up as he faced her. But she could see fear now and then lurking in those clear blue depths and around the edges of his voice even as he tried so hard to be a little man. She squatted on the back of her legs to be able to speak with him eye to eye.

"I see. And where is your mom?" Her gaze swiftly swung up and down the hallway and saw no sign of an accompanying adult.

"She died when I was real little."

Jamie's heart caught in her throat at that bit of information. That left the obvious that he got separated from someone who was probably searching for him that very moment. He was a lost little boy.

"I'm sorry you're lost. Tell me who you came here with,

and I'll see if we can find her for you."

"I'm not lost," he spoke up. "I know I'm here. My dad is here, too. But people said I was too little to come back here. I'm big for my age. My dad will be worried if he doesn't see me."

"Who brought you to the hospital?" She would try that tact one more time.

"Pops did, in his truck."

"Where is Pops now?"

"He had to park the truck."

"And how did you find your way back here?" Although the hospital was not large by most standards, it did take some maneuvering to find the entrance to the surgical wing. This little guy had managed to do so, and on his own. "Did Pops tell you to wait in the reception area for him?" By the telltale coloring that rose in his cheeks at her question, she had her answer.

"There you are! Andy, I told you to wait up front for me. You're going to give me a heart attack one of these days."

Jamie rose to stand, taking in the older man, dressed in faded, but clean denim jeans, his own sweat-coated hat carried by tobacco-stained fingers at his side, his hair, what little there was of it, grew in tufts of gray across the crown. Scuffed and worn-work boots still only brought him to an inch taller than her own height of five feet, five inches. His eyes reflected the fact he had weathered a lot of years, and probably many a bad road as evidenced by the lines radiating from their corners in a windblown, sun-speckled face that placed his age someplace north of sixty... Maybe even flirting with seventy.

"I'm sorry, ma'am, if he was bothering you. Sometimes I think I need to bring a rope just to tie him in one spot for more than two seconds."

Jamie could well imagine that this particular youngster could be a handful at times. She turned a professional smile on the older man. "He wasn't a bother. He was telling me he's looking for his father. Did you check at the front desk?"

"I didn't have that much time, once I discovered this one missing. But I do know he had surgery last evening right after he was brought in."

Jamie had just walked onto the floor right before the young man appeared, so she had not begun the shift meeting with the four other nurses who worked the surgery unit. She moved behind the console again and scanned the list of patients. Thomas Tremayne, Jr. was third on their short list.

"He's in Room 201, but I'm afraid the policy is that no children below the age of twelve are allowed in this wing." She saw the hint of a tremble at the corner of the mouth of the little boy before her. Again, there was that unfamiliar tug within her. Jamie's next words surprised even herself as they came out.

"If you'll both have a seat in those chairs in the waiting room behind you," her head nodded in that direction, "that will give me some time to check on Mr. Tremayne myself.

I'll come speak with you after that."

"Thank you very much, ma'am. We appreciate that. Come on, Andy, sit yourself." The pair moved to make themselves comfy in a pair of blue plastic chairs that no one would ever describe as comfortable.

Jamie walked down the hall and pushed open the door to the fourth room on the right. The blinds were drawn over the one large window in the room and the only light came from the fluorescent fixture above the bed. White blankets had evidently lost in a tug-of-war with the man beneath them and were shoved down past his waist. A swath of bandaging covered a good portion of his lower rib cage, a plastic ankle boot kept the sheeting raised from his lower left leg.

She moved closer and signed on to the computer terminal on the platform jutting from the wall beside the bed. Her eyes were soon scanning Dr. Cuesta's notes. The surgery had removed a foreign object—specified as a broken strip of metal fencing—from the ankle where it had lodged itself. It indicated need for monitoring for nerve damage and would have orders for future physical therapy. A couple of bruised ribs would require some mending time. The cuts and scrapes were superficial. All in all, nothing life-threatening, just aggravating to someone who obviously was involved in ranch work. Exiting from the record, she moved to stand closer to the head of the bed, her eyes observing the man and not the paperwork.

He spent his life in the outdoors as evidenced by the tanned skin of his upper body, muscled arms, and the planes of his face. It was a strong face. It was definitely one that you would notice…strong nose, square jaw covered in a couple of days' growth of stubble at the moment. Lowered lashes on his cheeks indicated he slept, and she momentarily wondered what color the eyes would be. His hair was a thick, dark chestnut color and looked as though it might be raked through by long fingers on a regular basis. Her gaze slid down to rest on the mouth. It was interesting and the lips definitely…

"Get me out of this bed." Those lips moved at that moment, and the voice they emitted was deep and none too soft. It was a coarse rumble that came from deep within the bandaged chest. This was followed by an immediate wince as his ribs had their say.

"Sorry, but you're our guest for a few days. I would suggest you not make any sudden moves or issue any more orders. Bruised ribs can be painful, especially if you keep irritating them with your loudness."

"I know all about hurt ribs. I had them before and I survived just fine."

Why was she not surprised he was going to be a difficult patient? "Then you know that the longer you disobey orders, the longer you suffer. But please, suffer in silence as there are other patients on this hall who are in worse shape than you."

His eyes came fully open and locked on her. She had an

answer to her earlier silent question… They were the same vivid blue as his son's. There could be no mistaking they were related. Also, no mistaking the electric effect they had on her ability to think clearly in that moment. They packed quite an unexpected punch, and she didn't care for its effect.

"That's some bedside manner. Thought nurses were supposed to be compassionate?"

"Thought cowboys had manners?" she came right back at him, finding control over her breathing again. "Guess there are exceptions to all rules."

She moved to the doorway and paused, looking over her shoulder at him. "By the way, your son is in the waiting room. I'm going to allow him two minutes in here, provided you calm down and keep your voice below a shout."

THOMAS'S EYES HELD the empty spot where she had stood for a full minute after she left. *Smart-mouthed little thing.* His eyes next moved to the ceiling. *Fine mess.* Here he was, stuck in a hospital bed, with a ranch to run and a son to keep an eye on, then add a cheeky nurse that looked at him with eyes that reminded him of a wounded doe he had come across last fall…all full of mistrust, a hint of fear, and still a will to fight all rolled into one. Large, sable-brown, expressive doe eyes. *Damn.* The pain meds must be playing with his brain.

He hadn't given much thought to any female for a long

time. Well, not *real* thought, he amended. There were the occasional "dates" he had every two or three weeks with that bank teller in the next county. That was just to fill a natural need they both had—she a widow of three years and he…well, he was a single dad of almost seven years. And he wasn't looking to be hooked again by *any* female. No matter what color her eyes. Once was more than enough for him.

The door opened, and those doe eyes were now shuttered and coolly professional. She gave a nod of her head behind her and the small form of his son came into view. The little boy halted beside the woman, his eyes going from the hospital bed to the woman's face. The man felt a quick stab somewhere above the damaged rib cage as he noted the way his son looked at the woman beside him and how magically, her face transformed with an almost ethereal light as an actual smile was bestowed on the youngster. Her voice was soft velvet, and he felt an odd moment of longing for it to be directed at him. *Get a grip. She's just doing her job.*

"Remember what I said about hugging. I'll come back for you shortly." She stood and watched the small figure move with solemn steps toward the man in the bed. Thomas raised his hand off the blanket, and the little boy's small hand grabbed for it as if it were a lifeline. The intensity of the smile that crossed the man's face went straight to the heart. She cleared her throat and stepped quickly from the room. Distance was needed from the pair.

"How are you and Pops doing?"

"We're okay, I guess, 'cept he forgot to put eggs in the pancakes, and they didn't taste good and they looked kinda funny. So we had toast. I like it with the black stuff on the edges."

Black stuff…great. He needed out of the hospital bed or his son would be treated to a lot of black stuff. He'd give Milton Lewis's sister a call and maybe she could pitch in with meals while he was stuck in the hospital. If he hadn't been in such a rush to get to the house and pack up his son for school yesterday morning, then he wouldn't be in this mess. His mind had not focused as it should have when they were moving the larger steers into the pens for the trucks. A fluke accident had him and his left side penned between two iron posts and the metal gate, and the posts won in the contest with his body.

He needed to make sure his son was taken care of. Pops had been the senior foreman of the Four T Land and Cattle Company since before he was born. He knew everything there was to know about cattle and ranching, but very little about children and dietary needs and all the rest of the things Thomas had had to learn quickly when his wife walked off without a backward glance when their son was barely three months old.

"You need to promise me that you'll mind Pops just like you always have, and do your chores and help take care of things until I get back, okay? Your aunt and uncles are busy and out on the road for a few more weeks, so we have to all pull together."

"Yes, sir. I promise. I'll take care of the ranch for you." His eyes were solemn.

Thomas Tremayne's heart swelled with pride as his hand rose to ruffle the sandy-colored hair visible now that his son held his hat in his hand at his side. Big Boss and Little Boss, as the ranch hands called them sometimes, had been a pair since the day when his son had reached out and with the smallest fingers in the world, curled them around his own small pinkie when the nurse handed him the swathed bundle. The tall cowboy and the baby looked at each other with solemn matching gazes for several long moments. A bond forged itself in blue steel in that short period of time and only grew stronger with each passing day.

"Nurse Jamie is nice." His son's words surprised the man. "She bended the rules so I could come visit you."

"Broke, not bended," he corrected his son. So the woman wasn't as ramrod stiff as he first thought? "We must thank her for that."

"I already did. And she gave me a lollipop, too. But she made me promise to not eat it until Pops said I could. I put it in my back pocket."

"Time is up, little man." Nurse Jamie walked into the room with a smile on her face…for the little boy. When her eyes lifted to the patient, the smile disappeared. "I believe your foreman wants a word. I gave him three minutes and then you need to rest." Her gaze returned to the boy as did the smile. Her hand reached out for his, and his small one automatically left his dad's and joined hers. Something akin to sadness smacked through the man's feelings at how easily his son had given his allegiance to the woman.

"Bye, Dad. Don't worry about us. See you later," his son tossed over his shoulder with a wide grin. Then he disappeared. The shuffling figure of Pops Turner entered next.

"Before you go getting yourself all worked up, let me tell you that Dottie said she would be glad to come over and make sure the kid doesn't starve. She'll be with him at the house until I get back in the evenings. Between us and the rest of the hands, we'll take care of the ranch and Andy, too. So don't lay around here worrying. We got it under control. And I already let your brothers and sister know what happened and that it's all taken care of. Little missy wanted to fly home right away. But I talked her out of it. I figured you'd not want any of them pulling off the circuit contracts because of a little dustup. Don't worry about your aunt, either. She's on that cruise ship and won't get wind of this."

"You got that right. Those contracts are what matters. And Aunt Sal hasn't had a vacation in a few years, and this isn't something she needs to worry about just three days into a month-long vacation to Europe. It's good to know that Dottie can help you out. I figured you'd be on top of things. I just know what a handful Andy can be these days."

"Over fifty years I've kept an eye on the ranch and you Tremaynes. It stops only when I'm six feet under. You should just enjoy this little vacation of your own for a while…and the scenery." The man's eyes had a sparkle of mischief coloring the last words.

"There's a scrawny bush and a brick retaining wall beyond my window, not much scenery."

Pops eyed him. "You've been around cows too long. I meant the scenery *inside* this hospital. You didn't hit your head, did you? That's a mighty pretty little thing that takes your temperature."

"That nurse is as prickly as a cactus and probably as ornery as the rattler you'd find coiled under it," Tom responded, not caring for the way the older man's eyes narrowed in on him. He was glad his foreman didn't reply. He didn't have time.

"Rattlers give a warning when they're about to strike. I don't." The words brought both men's gazes toward the door. "Your time is up, Pops." Jamie's eyes swung from the foreman to the patient. "And this is for you." The gleam of the hypodermic needle in her hand matched the wicked glint in her eyes.

Chapter Two

*F*OUR DAYS AND *it seems like forty.* That's how Jamie described her experience of the last few days with Thomas Tremayne, the second one, as a patient on her wing. While he frightened the younger, inexperienced nurses with his constant scowls and gruff tones, he had the three older nurses…older being in their mid- to late-thirties and divorcees…well, he had them madly in lust with him at first sight. And she had to deal with it all.

However, his disposition wasn't much better with the seasoned staff. Jamie found a new, perverse hint of enjoyment the times when she was able to poke or prod or stick the recalcitrant cowboy who was at her mercy. After the second day, he had grown quiet, allowing his gaze to watch her like a wary hawk as she flitted about his room, performing her duties.

While she maintained a professional demeanor in his presence, and among her coworkers, once she left the hospital confines, it was a different story. As much as Jamie tried to control her mind and keep the rancher away from her thoughts outside the building, her brain revolted and would not listen. That was a new wrinkle. She usually could leave her work and patients behind her, but for whatever reason, the rancher frustrated that pattern.

For the last fourteen years, she had made a life for herself since she stepped outside a courthouse at the age of sixteen. That life was ordered and safe and had walls around it as impenetrable as the Great Wall of China. No bad tempered, ill-mannered male was going to upset her well-ordered, quiet existence. That was one of the reasons she had chosen the small hospital in the county seat of Faris, Texas. Quiet was the order of the day. Now and then, emergencies would fill the small emergency wing, such as the three-car pileup on the nearby interstate last winter resulting from an ice storm. They had triaged and sent them on to a trauma unit via air evac helicopter to Lubbock. Occasionally there would be an accident in the oil fields or a ranch hand would get hurt. It wasn't the hurried pace of the big city trauma unit she had left in Dallas. And that was fine with her.

When Jamie had interviewed for the position, sixteen months ago, she had been told the one hundred and twenty bed hospital had been a charitable gift from a local ranching family to the citizens of Drake County. Most of Drake County was rural, mainly ranches and small farms, with Faris, and its population of 9,200 a shadow of its former self during the oil-field boom of previous decades. It had to reinvent itself like so many of the other Texas towns over the years.

The town council had played up its "quaintness" and empty buildings became antique-filled stores for weekend shoppers from the cities. Cute bed-and-breakfasts, country diners, and many other boutique-styled shops lured new business and life to the town. Yet, the residents were adamant in preserving the small-town, unhurried lifestyle for its inhabitants, most of whom were families with roots spread over many generations.

Jamie was fine with the slow pace, the quiet friendliness of the locals, and the lack of any major nightlife. For that, people either traveled the almost two hours into Austin or San Antonio. Or they could travel a half hour down the winding country road to McKenna Springs and take in the restaurants there and country music at the legendary Yellow Rose dance hall.

On her days off, she would occasionally take drives to other nearby towns or enjoy the country roads and beautiful Hill Country scenery. Jamie was practiced in being frugal from her childhood up to adulthood, and the savings she had tucked away allowed her to purchase a small two-bedroom frame house from one of the doctors on staff. It was tucked away on a side street behind the local Baptist church. All in all, it was a content life she had carved out for herself as the charge nurse for the surgery unit. If only Thomas Tremayne would hurry up and be released so her quiet life could continue.

If the people of Faris found it odd at first, that a young,

single woman of thirty, with above-average looks and intelligence, and no ties within the county would even consider a move to their distant community from the big city, few voiced any concerns. Her experience and hard work made her a welcome addition to the hospital staff and her compassion for the patients and their families had earned her warm respect in the almost year and a half she had been on the staff. Their friendliness had eased her first few months, and she had found a security in knowing people looked out for each other. That was something she was still trying to get used to. She had grown up in an atmosphere of constant distrust and upheaval. She had been determined to find a better way of life for herself and she had.

When Dr. Cuesta summoned her into his office that Monday morning, she should have known things were about to go from bad to worse where a certain patient was concerned. However, she was not prepared for her part in it.

"I don't think I heard you correctly." Jamie blinked a couple of times while she tried to clarify the physician's words in her mind. "Did you say that you want me to go home with that man and serve as his personal nurse…in his home?" Did her voice sound a bit shrill at the end of that sentence? Perhaps it sounded that way because she felt that way. She was glad of the chair under her. Her nails dug into the leather of the arms.

Dr. Cuesta was a kindly man in his early sixties and was the physician who had recruited her and hired her for the position she held. She had great respect for his work, except now she was in doubt of his sanity.

"I can't do that. I am the surgical charge nurse. I have duties here. I'm not a private-duty nurse. Surely, you can enlist a home health service from the county?"

"Of course, you are the charge nurse here. That position is yours, and we aren't about to lose you. But we can cover that for the time you would be needed elsewhere. The crux of this matter is that Mr. Tremayne needs help at home with monitoring his ankle injury and ensuring that he has the physical therapy twice a day that we think best. The county health service has no private-duty nurses available. And you know we are already short one physical therapist due to maternity leave. We can't spare the other two. But you are aware that he is not the most helpful of patients. He's already gotten up and out of bed on that ankle and made us have to go back and redo our work.

"We're certainly not overcrowded on the surgical wing at the moment. You've had experience with rehab patients also. If we can provide assistance to the Tremayne family, we'll do so. This community and this hospital owe a great deal to them. Without their family's generosity, you and I would not be having this conversation, because there would be no hospital in this community. Do you see my point?"

The light dawned bright. It was crystal clear to her. The Tremaynes were the donors that gave the community its hospital. They were *owed*, and this was one way in which Dr.

Cuesta saw to repay their generosity, except *she* was now part of the repayment plan. By the same token, she also knew she owed the hospital for taking a chance on a young nurse from the city. But being in that cowboy's debt was not the place she preferred to be.

"The Tremaynes would never parlay anything they do as making them special enough to expect favors or anything along those lines. They never have. And I will share with you that this request did not come from Thomas Tremayne. He fought it. It came via a phone call from Sallie Lomax. She's Thomas's aunt and a major contributor in her own right, as she owns a business here in Faris and sits on several community boards, including ours. But she is very concerned over his health and ability to adhere to what he needs to do to heal properly once out of the hospital. She asked a favor of me as a friend and concerned relative. How she deals with Thomas on the issue is her concern, and I am staying away from that hot potato. If she were here and not out of the country, this would be a moot point. I hope I can count on you to understand the assignment."

"I'm beginning to get a clearer picture. And I can't say that her concerns about the patient's behaving are unfounded after dealing with him as I have."

The man smiled at her response. "Now that Thomas has capitulated to his aunt, he is looking at the situation with more calm after the phone call. I can also add that he realizes this is asking a great deal of you and is graciously making a donation to cover your salary while on leave from your duties here, and to also provide a very nice bonus for yourself, as well." Dr. Cuesta was very pleased with delivering that last bit of news. Then he grinned. "He referred to it as 'hazard pay.' He figured you'd appreciate that."

I bet he did. Jamie knew that sealed her fate. If she refused, she would be placing the hospital in a bad light with their benefactors. She would also pique interest in why she would not be agreeable to receiving such compensation for what sounded like very light duty. The last thing she wanted or needed was to have people's interest aroused by anything involving her. Over the years, she had cultivated being the person who fit seamlessly into the background, never calling attention to herself. She needed to put aside her misgivings and keep in mind this was her duty to get the patient situated and on the road to health again. *Some patient. He was irritable and full of himself on the best day.*

"We plan to release him tomorrow afternoon. I would have sent him home already except for the fact I know the man would not have followed the care regimen needed from the get-go. Getting you in place for his dismissal is the best way to handle the situation." The doctor continued without any verbal agreement needed from her. "You can take your things out to the ranch this afternoon and get settled in. There's a small boy, his son, but I believe you met him already. However, he isn't your concern."

"I'll do my best." She was slow to reach the door. Her

mind tried to find one last reason but came up short of a way out of the temporary assignment.

"I know you will. Think of it as a mini vacation. You'll have time in your day to enjoy some fresh air. Take along a good book or two. I'll be in touch by phone daily should you need anything."

Vacation…right. Jamie repeated the word as two hours later, with luggage in the trunk of her small car, the exercise regimen and schedule from the physical therapist in the folder beside her, she left the town behind her. Her mood was the only dark spot on a cloudless blue-sky day, as she followed the GPS along the designated route. Fifteen minutes from town, she turned off the main interstate onto a smaller two-lane blacktop heading westward between twin hills. In the distance, she saw the rising form of the lone flat-topped mesa that, according to her directions, sat with the ranch at its base. However, it was still several miles away. The air was warming, but pleasantly so. Jamie let it blow through the car from her open window, preferring it to the car's air-conditioning. The calendar showed it was late spring. But in the state of Texas, Mother Nature played by her own rules. The mornings were chilly enough to still call for a light wrap. The afternoon heat shimmered across the land and made one look forward to a dip in the cold rivers of the area. Evenings were a toss-up. It pleased her to see that there were still a few late blooming bluebonnets waving their blue sea of petals in the never-ceasing breezes.

The next thing that came into view was the simple black iron arched gateway heralding her arrival at the Four T Land and Cattle Company. It was framed on one side by the flag of the Lone Star State, and on the other by the Stars and Stripes. Another sign pointed to the road to her left and stated that the entrance to the Four T Rodeo Stock Ranch was another half mile down the blacktop. She glanced at her directions again and made the turn toward the Land and Cattle Company. A black metal mailbox stand fitted with a half-dozen mailboxes attached to it stood to one side. The heavy-looking metal gate was wide open, and her car bounced over the iron gratings of the cattle guard, producing a loud clanging sound as the car bounced over the metal.

The paved road continued across a bridge over a dry creek bed, around a few more curves and over another couple of arroyos before the pens and covered barns came into view. Per the written instructions, Jamie continued on the same road, passing the outer buildings with their metal roofs reflecting the afternoon sun. She passed a rock home that was evidently several years old judging by the established shade trees and landscaping. The main house was just ahead, and she slowed, pulling to a stop at the sidewalk leading from the circular driveway. The house was long with a wide porch that ran its length. The second story also had a veranda that did the same. The white stone and oak trim complemented the whole setting. The lawn had a mixture of younger trees and a couple of large, older oak trees. The grass was beginning to turn to the light green stems that would lend itself to a thicker dark green coating as the days progressed. The walkway was dotted on each side by a mixture of wild sage plants and rose bushes that had yet to bloom. It all had the look of an oasis in a vast sea of browns and red clays.

Turning off her engine, Jamie gathered her folder and slipped her bag over her shoulder. The slamming of the screen door on the wide porch brought her attention to the house as she opened the car door. A familiar small figure bolted across the porch and down the steps toward her, followed by a dog right on his heels. As she stood, she wondered if the child was going to be able to stop his flight before mowing her down. Instinctively, Jamie put out her hands to aid in this, but he braked just in time, a mile-wide smile on his face.

"You're here! I'm glad. Do you like horses? I have a horse. We put you in the room for special people. Do you like flowers? It has purple flowers on the wall. And this is Jasper. He's a really good dog. Do you like dogs? I hope so."

Jamie couldn't help but laugh at the mile a minute welcome.

"Let the lady have time to speak, boy." Pops and an older woman had come outside behind the fleeing pair and stood at the top of the steps, smiling. "Welcome to the Four T, Miss Westmoreland. We'll get the boys to get your stuff up to your room, but come in out of the sun and make yourself at home." He nodded at the two men who had come across the stable yard after her arrival.

Andy fell into step beside her, his grin as infectious as the first time she had seen it. If there was any upside to this assignment, it was the fact that she would be able to visit with this precocious and instantly likable child again. Perhaps it would make the whole event progress faster.

Think positive.

"This here is Dottie Lewis, she's our nearest neighbor. She's been looking in on the boy and making sure the food is edible," Pops said by way of introduction as she topped the porch. The older woman stepped forward with an outstretched hand and a warm smile.

"It's a pleasure to meet you. Although I've seen you a time or two in town. Once when I visited a friend in the hospital and once at the grocery store. I should have introduced myself one of those times and been more neighborly. I apologize it's taken a while to welcome you." Her gray eyes were kind and sincere and her handshake firm. Jamie judged her age to be close to Pop's.

She stood maybe a head taller than the man beside her. Tall, with salt-and-pepper hair cut in a short, no-nonsense fashion, she wore a light blue sweater, jeans, and the prerequisite boots. Jamie liked her open, friendly manner. It was much the same as what she had encountered from many of the rest of the townspeople along the way. What you saw was what you got…no pretensions.

"It's a pleasure," Jamie responded and noted that Andy had scooted ahead of them with a quiet Jasper and stood holding the front door wide for her to enter. She stepped across the threshold and was immediately struck by a wonderful smell of fresh-baked bread. If the smell was any indication, the food was definitely edible. She had a quick impression of large open rooms with heavy oak furniture, leather couches, and western paintings…a man's domicile. It was functional, heavy, and without color…just a continuation of browns and beiges from the outside.

"I'll show you to your room and let you get settled. I usually come back around five and put a casserole in the oven. Ted comes up and takes over when he gets in from the barns. It's the weekend, so Andy is in and out with him or around the yards with Jasper." Dottie turned at the bottom of the stairs and spoke to the young boy about to follow them. "Never mind, young man. You get back to the kitchen and finish your sandwich and milk. Let Miss Jamie have some quiet to get settled. Run on…"

Andy wasn't happy about this turn of events, but he did as he was told, a slow shuffle in his steps.

Dottie chuckled softly as she led the way upstairs. "That one is a handful of energy, but he's a good boy. He's been told why you're here and he'll be a help to you—showing you where things are and all that. Sometimes I forget he's almost seven because he acts a lot older in many ways. He hasn't been babied as most children in their first seven years of life, but that's Thomas's business and not mine. He's done a good job for a single parent. But it'll be nice for Andy to have a younger female in the house, even for a short while."

This bit of news had come as a surprise to Jamie when she had first heard it...from gossip between the other two nurses in their breakroom when they learned she would be working with their prize patient in his home. They had quickly informed her that Thomas Tremayne, and his two brothers, were the prize bachelors in several counties. The family owned a huge amount of land that had lots of cattle and the best part according to them, a few oil wells to sweeten the deal, too. Plus, *they* considered this Tremayne to be gorgeous and sexy due to his aloofness, having sidestepped many matrimonial traps set by females over the years.

That's where the story got murky when it came to why there was no Mrs. Tremayne in the picture. One rumor was that she had died years before in childbirth. Another rumor had it that she left the ranch one day and never was seen again. Jamie didn't care which was true. All she cared about was that she wanted to get the job done and be rid of the patient that had compared her to a prickly cactus and creepy reptile. He could keep his brooding good looks and sarcastic jibes for those females who found that sort of thing attractive...along with his oil wells and cows. He was a man, and men were often more trouble than they were worth. Few of them earned her trust. She learned early on in life that only she could take care of herself.

Jamie's room turned out to be a two-room suite with its own bath. There was a small sitting room with a comfy-looking chair and ottoman next to the wide window with light lace curtains that overlooked the front yard, a small settee and table with lamp and a bookshelf. The bedroom had a lovely, antique-looking four-poster bed with a quilt of lavenders, yellows, and cream squares. The purple flowers Andy had mentioned earlier were in reality tiny lavender flowers on the antique cream wallpaper. The polished wooden floor had a couple of cream throw rugs on it and a matching dresser and mirror completed the room. The bath was modern with a tub/shower combination. Just as the downstairs, the room was nice but minimally furnished in comparison to most homes of the same size. Jamie was okay with it. She wasn't there to be a guest or to spend a lengthy amount of time.

"The house has internet and cable. There's a landline phone in the kitchen, too. Maria Aguilar, she's married to Ted's assistant, Daniel Aguilar, comes over in the mornings now and fixes breakfast for Andy. She lives in a house on the ranch about a quarter mile from here—close to the show barns you saw on your drive in. She's expecting her third child, so she moves a bit slow, but she is a sweet person and you'll like her. She's at her prenatal checkup or she'd be here to meet you.

"Her number is posted next to the phone in the kitchen,

next to mine and Ted's cell number and Thomas's, too. Don't hesitate to call any of us if you need anything."

Jamie had to interrupt. "I'm sorry, Dottie. Forgive me, but I'm a bit confused by something. You keep referring to someone named Ted. I don't…"

"Oh my goodness." Dottie laughed, shaking her head. "Forgive me for that one. You see I know Pops by his given name of Ted, short for Theodore. I've been in the habit for many years of calling him that name. I forget that might sound strange to those who don't know the background."

"That explains it. I understand. I'm sorry I interrupted you, please go on."

"Well, I come in at noon with lunch and come back at five for dinner. As Ted said, my brother Milton and I are the closest neighbors. We live eight miles in the opposite direction from where you turned off from the interstate to get here, so about twenty miles as the crow flies," she finished with a half laugh.

"You drive back and forth each day like that? It takes a chunk of your day," Jamie commented.

"Well, that's what neighbors do for each other. Thomas would do the same…and has…for Milt and me. Especially when my husband fell off a dang windmill about four years back and ended up dying on us. He was laid up for a while before he died, and Thomas and his siblings along with Ted were right there to help out every day. He may not show it much to strangers, but Thomas Tremayne is a fine and decent man and would give you the shirt off his back if you needed it. All of the Tremaynes would. Just don't tell him I said so. He likes to make people think he's not a softy."

"I would never think that," Jamie said with tongue in cheek. He was certainly not a softy in her eyes. And she would never expect anything of him besides what she had already received…a headache and heightened stress at having to take on the assignment to begin with.

"Andy will finish his lunch and then he can show you the rest of the house. He has the run of the main ranch area…the houses, barns, pens. He knows the rules about what areas to stay clear of without his dad or Ted with him, such as the bull area, stock pens, etcetera. Jasper is his constant companion outside and inside, and he keeps his eyes on the boy. He grabbed him by the seat of his diaper a time or two over the years. That dog is a smart one. I swear he could be human at times.

"On weekdays, Thomas usually takes Andy to school in the mornings on his way into town for supplies or coffee at the diner or things like that. Then Maria brings him home after school with her. She works as a part-time aide at the school. Her two children are in a grade ahead of Andy. Course, I don't know what we'll do now that Thomas is out of commission. We'll have to work on that one. I hear the boys coming upstairs with your luggage. You come down to the kitchen when you're ready." Dottie left her alone to settle in.

Dottie talked a mile a minute and Jamie had a lot to digest. She liked the older woman. And Pops was nice, too...a bit crusty around the edges at times but that was to be expected of a man who spent his entire life around cattle and not so much around people. *"Salt of the earth."* That was a term she had heard more than once since arriving in this part of West Texas. She had met very few people in her life that term could be used to describe...very few indeed. In fact, Jamie had met the opposite kind.

She had seen the darkest in human nature and would never forget it. It was only in the last couple years—mainly since coming upon Faris, Texas—that she began to allow herself to actually open the door to trusting a select number of people. And very few of the male variety, really only one when she actually thought about it, Dr. Cuesta. Jamie took it one day at a time. One day, maybe she wouldn't look back over her shoulder at strangers, or scan strange cars driving too slowly in the neighborhood. It was trusting members of the opposite sex which might never happen again. But she pushed those thoughts into the box in the corner of her mind where they were best kept.

A HALF HOUR later, Jamie stood at the top of the steps on the wide porch. Andy stood next to her, and Jasper sat next to him. They raised a wave in answer to the one tossed their way as Dottie turned her truck in the direction of the main gate and left them. A brisk breeze rose off the flat land to the southwest and Jamie pulled the soft jacket closer around her. Andy had a jean jacket on along with his usual western shirt and jeans, boots, and the huge cowboy hat. In fact, the only time she had seen him without the hat had been beside his father's bed in the hospital on his first clandestine visit and earlier in the kitchen while he sat at the table and ate his lunch.

Jamie's gaze took in the wide-open spaces around them. You could see for miles in all directions…unless there was a tall mesa in the way like the one that rose behind the house. Growing up, she'd been a city girl, having been raised in Dallas and then Houston. She hadn't known there was land like this until she was a teenager. And yet, instead of being foreign to her, she found she had come to prefer the openness. You could see the stars in the sky at night and watch the storm clouds roll in across the distance. The air was fresh and clean. The people were open and honest. There was plenty of room to get lost in, and you could see trouble coming before it was too late.

"Let's go to the barn and you can meet my horse," Andy piped up.

"Not so fast," she replied as she smiled down at him, not wanting to dampen his enthusiasm. "How about I learn about this house first? I need to do that so I can help your dad when he comes home tomorrow."

Andy considered this and found its importance was worthy of preempting a visit to the barn. He nodded his head. "Okay." He went into tour guide mode.

Besides the obvious living room to the right of the foyer, there was the formal dining room where Andy pointed out "we eat in here when special people come." Moving through the large kitchen with its wide countertops and cast iron cookware, they stepped into a hallway that opened into a den area that was a mixture of things…a cluttered desk and chair, bookshelves, a big-screen television, a couple of overstuffed chairs, and lots of stacks of books and magazines and paper. A small bath was located just beyond it with a shower stall.

"This is where I watch TV and my dad works on papers and stuff," Andy explained in his matter-of-fact tour guide voice. "No one really comes back here 'cept for us. He has another office down by the cattle barns, but he sits in here so we can talk and stuff. And now you can sit in here, too."

She doubted that would happen, but she had to admit it was nice the man took time to spend with his son instead of locked away in another building in the evenings. Up the back stairs from the kitchen, she found herself in the hall that led to the right and to her suite. To the left, they came to Andy's room. It had light blue walls with posters and photos of horses and rodeo cowboys. Bookshelves held books with horse themes and other shelves held a couple of board games and drawing items. The bunk bed caught her attention. It had been specifically built to resemble a corral of some sort. Andy saw her face.

"It's an awesome bed. My uncle Truitt built it for me last year. It looks like a rodeo chute and there's a desk underneath and the bed on top."

"I must say I have never seen a bed like that one. Your uncle is very talented, and he must really like you a lot." She smiled at the child. The dark blue covers and beige pillows matched the blue curtains covering the window. There was a closet that through the half open door, Jamie could see the collection of western wear and a couple of pairs of boots. A black felt hat rested on a top shelf. There were no baseball mitts, footballs, caps, or sneakers one would expect to find in a little boy's domain. All cowboy gear. A bathroom was attached through a side door.

The door at the end of the hall opened into the master suite. It was large…and dark. The shades were closed. The light switch illuminated a sitting room with beige carpet on the floor, and a couple of Navajo-style throw rugs on top of it. Two leather chairs sat in front of the fireplace that had obviously held no fire in a while. A shirt had casually been tossed on the arm of one chair. A pair of work boots sat on the floor next to it. There were bookshelves with lots of books—mostly ranching tomes and a few biographies thrown in. Through an archway, a huge four-poster bed filled the space, this one immense in carved wood and covered in a deep brown suede comforter. Jamie's gaze skipped onward. She noted a walk-in closet and large bath to the left. This would be Thomas Tremayne's lair and his abode beginning tomorrow. Her mind tried to imagine him in it, and she shut the door firmly on that for the time being. As she turned to leave the room, her gaze fell on a framed photograph sitting on top of the chest. It showed a smiling and large family. She saw Thomas; he was holding a small baby in his arms, which had to be Andy, she guessed. There was a couple who resembled the younger members in the photo and those had to be Thomas's parents. Thomas resembled his dad quite a bit. The woman had a warm and friendly smile. Then there were three other younger men and a little girl. They looked like a happy group. They looked like people she might have liked to know. A fanciful thought that was new to her. She shut off the light and closed the door behind them.

There were two other smaller bedrooms upstairs. But it was clear that they had not been in use for some time. Their tour concluded on the back porch and to Jamie's surprise, there was a patio with a BBQ pit built into the half wall, and then on the next level, a swimming pool sat with a cover stretched in place over it. There was a large hot tub beside it…also covered.

"I bet you enjoy that pool in the summer," she remarked to her young companion.

"I can only go in it with my dad. And he's busy a lot. We can turn the heater thing on and it warms up so we can swim longer when we want. And sometimes we go swimming and fishing in this really neat part of the river that runs through the ranch." Jamie didn't have time to digest much more. "Now can we go to the barns?"

"Okay," she capitulated with a smile. He had been far more patient than she imagined he would be on the tour. Jamie was rewarded with a mega-watt grin in return.

"Yippee!" He would have raced ahead but he tried to slow down to her pace. It was obviously hard for him. The barn was a short distance from the house. It was huge and the doors were open; there was some activity inside. The two "boys"—as Dottie had referred to them—had come to the house, been introduced to her, and carried in her luggage. They were actually two men, one in his mid-forties and the other perhaps in his late twenties…Don and Leroy. Right now, they were busy saddling a couple of horses. They nodded at her entrance.

Don spoke up. "What are you up to, Andy?"

"I'm showing Nurse Jamie my horse." He headed to a stall where a large head moved over the top and greeted him with a snort.

"Mind you don't take him out of the stall…and you don't go inside," Don reminded him with a nod to Jamie and a wink. It was obvious these guys all considered themselves surrogate uncles to this little boy. The two cowboys led their horses out of the barn with a tip of their hats in her direction. They had cast appreciative glances her way when they'd been introduced but were mannerly, and she did not feel threatened in any way. She had to get used to the fact that there were indeed some gentlemen in the world…especially in this corner of it.

"I know," Andy replied, moving a step stool in front of the gate and stepping up on it. The horse reached his head farther over the barrier in order to allow the small hand to reach his nose.

Jamie smiled at the picture it made—the small cowboy and the large animal. Although she supposed in comparison to the two horses that the cowboys had just saddled and led outside, this one might be a tad bit smaller. He wasn't a pony necessarily, but not overly huge, either. She stepped slowly forward.

"This is Red Bug. Dad gave him to me for Christmas this year. I ride him when Dad is here with me. Before that, I got to ride with him on his horse, Enforcer, or on one of the ponies in the side corral. But Red Bug is a real horse and he's mine. You can pet him if you want."

Jamie eased a hand forward and felt the side of the soft nose. The large eyes gazed calmly at her. In fact, she could swear they held a smile as she ventured a rub along the sleek nose. "He feels like velvet. You are quite a nice horse, Red Bug."

"Dad'll get you a horse and you can come riding with us," Andy ventured, a smile lighting his face as the thought came to him. "We have lots of them."

"I don't think so, Andy," she responded. "Your dad

won't be doing any riding until he heals more. And I won't be around that long. I have a job at the hospital that needs me."

His face was crestfallen, and Jamie's heart responded. "The sooner we can get your dad feeling better, the sooner you and he can go back to riding together. And you'll be a big help to me in doing that. Can I count on your help?"

Andy replied with a smile and a nod of his head. "I can help you with my dad."

Jamie would need all the help she could get when his dad arrived tomorrow. She had no doubt about that.

Chapter Three

MIDMORNING NEXT DAY, Jamie stood on the steps of the main ranch house, a feeling of trepidation rolling around in the pit of her stomach. Andy and Jasper stood at the foot of the steps, anticipation in their every line. Pops had gone to the hospital to pick up the patient and had called to alert them that they had passed through the ranch gates a few minutes ago. Jamie tried to still the way her nerves had zinged on end at the news. She schooled herself to keep her professional mask in place and not let the man get a rise out of her. He was a *job*...pure and simple.

She had no idea if she would pull that off or not. After the barn tour yesterday, she had readied the house for his arrival—moved objects out of the way of the invalid and his crutches; straightened and then rearranged bedrooms; opened the blinds and let sunshine stream into the rooms, which led to dusting, and plumping of pillows. That led to Andy's exuberant assistance.

Jasper parked in the doorway and just watched. Jamie had to admit that the dog, an Australian cow dog, she had been informed, was a good companion. His coat was a shiny and slightly shaggy mixture of black and white and browns. He had one brilliant blue eye and one amber-colored eye that set him apart. They were quite striking along with the mouth that seemed in a perpetual smile.

Jamie had debated what to wear. Dress in jeans or slacks? Wear her usual hospital scrubs? Change the hair style? Or not… Then she had banged the closet door closed. How ridiculous was she being? She was a professional, employed to do a job. Jamie caught her just past shoulder length mahogany-brown hair back from her face in its usual smooth ponytail. A light hand in the makeup department and a pair of dark blue scrubs and her black oxfords completed the ensemble. She was there to work in her medical capacity.

The white ranch SUV with the Four T brand on its doors pulled up and parked in the driveway. Andy went forward to try to help with his dad's door. Jamie came down the steps after him. Pops came around and opened the back door, taking out a pair of crutches. The passenger door opened, and Andy gave a shout of happiness. With the help of a strong pair of hands, he managed to climb up and give a hug to his dad. Only Pops and Jamie saw the wince that crossed the brows of the man as he held his son for a moment.

"Okay, little man, let Dad try to get out of this truck," Jamie said.

Thomas let his son slide back to the ground. His gaze moved to lock on Jamie's. A half twist moved the corners of his mouth.

"Nurse Westmoreland...I trust you've made yourself at home?" His tone was just short of sarcastic.

"As this is not my home, I would not presume to do that. But I have your room ready for your arrival," she spoke briskly, a measured tone in her voice and eyes. "Please swing your legs out first. Carefully." She stepped forward, all business and in charge. Pops stood back and watched in silence. "Andy you may go up to the front door and wait until we need you to open it." He flew to take his position. "Place your left hand on the top of the door and your right on Pop's arm...then stand slowly...let your weight rest on the right foot...not the left."

"I think I can manage to get out of a car. Just give...*damn!*" The patient sank back against the SUV's seat. He had moved too quickly and had not listened about the weight distribution. The pain in his foot and ribs punished him. Jamie stood quietly, arms folded...waiting.

"Let's try it again...my way."

The look he threw at her would have cowed many a ranch hand in his vicinity. But it bounced off her without leaving a mark. He glared. She waited. He followed her instructions. Once he was standing, the crutches went under his armpits, and he actually began the slow process of moving up the walk. With Pops on one side, Jamie took the crutches at the bottom of the steps and moved ahead. She instructed him to place his free hand on the railing and take it one step at a time. The going was slow, and he halted a time or two to try to straighten and ease pressure on his ribs. He finally made it inside the house. With a supreme effort, he headed for the staircase.

"Where do you think you're going?" Jamie stepped forward.

"My bedroom."

"It will be easier for you downstairs for a little while. I had Don and Leroy move one of the single beds into the room you call a den. That keeps you on one floor and not having to deal with those stairs for a while."

"You moved me into the den?"

"Good. There's nothing wrong with your hearing. Follow me and let's get you in bed." She headed in the direction of the den. He was left to follow or not. He followed…gritting his teeth and mouthing some words under his breath.

Jamie was certain they were far from complimentary and aimed at her. But she didn't care. He was the patient and she was in charge…for the time being.

Thomas made it to the den and halted inside the doorway. The room had been cleaned and rearranged. His desk and chair sat next to the wide window—its blinds were open and sunlight filtered into the room and across the polished wood floor. The two chairs and ottomans had been pushed toward the fireplace, and the television had been mounted above it. The single bed was against the far wall with a bedside table and lamp. There were no obstacles to hinder his crutches.

"My clothes…" he began.

"Are in the hall closet off the bathroom right through that door." She nodded in the direction. "But you won't have need of a lot of them. Pajama bottoms with the leg cut up one side will suffice. You don't need anything to restrict your movements as regular clothing would."

"I'm not sitting around in pajamas during the day…even if I had a pair. I don't sleep in anything," he ground out.

"It's pajamas or a hospital gown…your choice. And Pops picked up a pair of pajamas in your size in town yesterday." If he thought he would embarrass her with the information about not sleeping in anything, then he was sorely out of luck. She might not be a chess player, but she could hold her own with most in a game of checkers.

She did not flinch at the firestorm in his blue eyes as they drilled into her. "You're working for *me*. I give the orders around here."

"I work for the hospital. They are trusting me to do my job, whether I am in the hospital or in this private home. However, I would be happy to return to my duties there and one of the other nurses could take my place," she offered with a swift half smile.

His gaze sharpened on her. His hands tightened on the crutches. "Has anyone ever mentioned you might try a person's patience?"

"You can't leave!" Andy piped up at that moment from the doorway. His eyes flew to his father's. "Dad, you said Nurse Jamie would come home with us. You promised."

Jamie's mind was on alert now. She watched the look passing between father and son. What promise had been made? And why? Several moments passed. Pops excused himself.

A deep sigh was visible along the wide shoulders of the man. "I may have spoken harshly…sorry. We don't need any other nurse in here." This brought immediate smiles of relief from his son. It was evident an apology did not come easily to the man.

"Andy, you need to wash up for Marcos's birthday party. Mrs. Aguilar will be here to pick you up soon," his father reminded him.

"I can stay and help you if you want." Andy looked up at Jamie.

"Every assistant needs time off. Go and have fun. We'll manage while you're gone." Jamie smiled at him. This smile was warm and transformed her face. It wasn't lost on the man.

"Okay!" The boy was gone in an instant, Jasper on his heels.

"Let's get you in bed. You've moved enough for a while." She was back to her efficient mode.

He moved to the bedside and eased himself down on its edge. It was clear he didn't like showing weakness in front of anyone...least of all her.

Jamie took the crutches and leaned them beside the head of the bed. She bent down and with deft fingers, removed the house slipper from his right foot. She stood up. "Can you manage your shirt, or do you want me to help?"

He looked at her for a second or two. His eyes shuttered their thoughts. "I think you need to help."

Jamie clamped her teeth together and said nothing. She kept her eyes on each button of his shirt front. All the while she was aware of the intensity of his gaze boring into her forehead. She dared not look up. The last button undone, she carefully moved her hands along the tops of his shoulders and lifted the material off and down his arms. His skin was smooth and the warmth from it seeped into her palms. Jamie knew that if she stopped for very long in one spot, it might even be hot enough to burn her. *Stop being so dramatic.*

As she raised her head, she thought she caught a glimpse of a mocking glint in his eyes. Was he laughing at her? Had he been aware of her reaction to removing his shirt? Was he toying with her? No man was going to make her feel inferior ever again. She straightened her back and met his gaze straight on.

"Let's get something straight right now." Her voice was low, but it meant business. "I'm here in a professional capacity, to do a job that Dr. Cuesta expects me to do. I will do it to the best of my ability. I am not here for your personal amusement in any way, shape or form. Do I make myself clear?"

Chapter Four

IN THE DEN, Tom slept fitfully. His mind wouldn't shut down. There was a problem and he couldn't wrap his brain around it. Actually, there was more than one problem, but Nurse Westmoreland was smack dab in the middle of all of them. She had rounded on him and put him in his place from the moment he arrived.

Maybe it was stupid of him to pull the bit about his shirt and the pajama remark, but he wanted to get a rise and find a crack in that smug, self-sufficient attitude of hers. But the look in her brown eyes had been almost pure fire. That the warning she had issued was the real thing registered immediately with him. Her response had taken him aback. Why she would have reacted that way, he had no idea. Maybe he shouldn't have noticed the faint blush in her cheeks as she took off his shirt. And maybe he shouldn't have asked her to do it when he could have done so.

Why he had deliberately pressed her buttons, he hadn't worked that out yet. Maybe it was to see again the way the golden sparks shot off in those eyes that turned from brown to a rich caramel when she turned them in his direction after he had done something to tee her off. Or the way her obstinate chin would raise ever so slightly when she addressed him…usually right after he had made a fool of himself in front of her. And what was that about? He didn't usually feel foolish in front of women. But this one had a way of making him feel that way with the merest lift of a delicate eyebrow.

However, there seemed to be some invisible barrier or a warning that shouted not to come too close or else suffer the consequences. Thomas didn't care for the way she had him second-guessing each thing he said or did around her. He was off-balance because of the accident. He had a ranch to run, responsibilities to the business that he and his siblings had worked hard to build up to be a national contender on the pro rodeo circuit. And he had a son to raise. There wasn't time to waste being an invalid.

Thomas sat upright against his pillows…something that was no small feat at the moment. Things were getting out of his control, in his own backyard. Andy was totally smitten with Nurse Jamie, as he had taken to calling her since the first meeting at the hospital. That meant when she left, he would know that heartbreak. It was something he had kept from his son's world. He hadn't been old enough to go through it with his mother's abandonment.

The family had banded together to shield Andy and supply more than enough love and care as he grew. But Thomas feared that sooner or later, that might not be enough when he started missing a mother figure in his world. Was that already happening with the nurse's appearance in their lives? He had tried to fill both sets of shoes as one parent and it wasn't enough. Maybe he was placing blame on the nurse where it didn't belong. *Maybe.* And maybe there was something else. He had faced the fact that he was mortal. What if things had gone differently with the pen accident? One wrong move on a ranch that kept animals that could easily maim…even kill…and a man could end up seriously injured or even dead. And where did that leave his son? He had made the usual stipulations on paper with his will and all, but in actuality, who would become the mainstay of his life and raise him? Had he been wrong in keeping another parent-figure from Andy's life? But he wasn't looking for someone to fill an empty role. He wanted what his parents had and that wasn't easy to find. Why the image of Jamie Westmoreland appeared in the corner of his brain at odd times only confused him all the more.

Lying in the hospital the last five days, he found that he actually looked for an excuse to have her step into his room. He was aware of the other nurses being more than anxious to step in and help out. But it was the brown-eyed head nurse that he kept finding his mind drifting toward…much to his aggravation. If he weren't an invalid, he would go find Nurse Westmoreland and have a few words. But what words? He was experiencing things that he didn't want to experience. What had gotten into him?

He had let one woman tie him into knots once upon a time and look where that ended. The harsh memory subsided as the smile of his son filtered through his mind. Only one thing good came from his brief marriage to Casey Hightower...his son. When she left them—with a pocketful of his money—she had left behind the child and a piece of paper giving up any rights to him. It was a moot point, given her death two years later in a plane crash in California. Andy knew none of the details, only that she had died. One day he would tell him the rest, but not for many years still to come. They had made a life together. They didn't need any woman coming in and messing it up. At least that was his previous thinking.

"I saw that grimace. It's time for another pain pill." The voice came from the woman who stepped out of his thoughts and stood watching him from the doorway. "I'll get one."

"I don't want a..." he began, but he let it go because she'd disappeared before hearing his disagreement. Why had he given in when Andy had begged to have Nurse Jamie be the nurse to come with them when he heard the doctor state that his dad would be released but needed some in-home care? *Right*...the woman didn't want to be here anymore than he wanted her there. But she was doing her duty. He had to give her that. She was dedicated to her work. Especially when it came to poking him with needles or other uncomfortable items.

She came back into the room, stopping beside the bed

and holding out a glass of water in one hand and a small white paper container with a pill inside on the other outstretched palm. She waited with calm authority. He hesitated but realized it would be easier to give in. He took the glass and the pill, downing them both. She took the empty glass back.

"Satisfied?"

"Yes, I am. I'm always pleased when patients do the smart thing for their healing. There's a casserole in the oven. When Andy gets back, I'll get your dinner ready. Until then, you should let the pill ease you into a nap." She went to turn away and then turned back. "I almost forgot. Your sister called earlier, on the landline. She was afraid you might be asleep, so she didn't try your cell phone. Although she did leave a message for you. Let's see, I need to get this right... *Tell my hard-headed, clumsy big brother to leave my bulls alone and stay out of their pen. And he better make sure that pen is repaired by the time I get back. And I love him.* That's the message."

"That sounds like Tori. Thanks for delivering the message. I can see that you relished getting it just right."

"I think your sister sounds like a very smart member of your family."

"I can just imagine why. And thanks for getting the love part there at the end right, too. I can imagine that was the hard part to remember."

That actually brought the first sign of a real smile from

her that was directed at him. And he coughed...when he took in a rush of air at the suddenness of the sight and choked.

"I don't have siblings, but I can imagine that it's nice to have someone else thinking about your welfare. Does she live far away? And your two brothers?"

Were they having something akin to a normal conversation? He was hesitant to do something to mess it up. "Not all that far. She moved into a house on the ranch where we have our rodeo stock headquarters...about five miles from here. She's an independent little spitfire. You two might get along just fine at that. My two brothers are busy with rodeo business, too. When they're home and not on the road, they live at the main ranch house along with our aunt Sallie who just started on a European cruise...her first vacation in years."

"Main house? This isn't the main ranch?"

"The Four T is basically two sections. The south portion, which is where you are right now, is the cattle operation. That's how the Tremaynes began way back in the 1800s...as ranchers. The last few years—those of us who are left—well, we branched out into raising rodeo stock that seems to have now moved into a successful rodeo producing business. That's why my sister and brothers are more like seasonal visitors it seems. Rodeo season is heating up."

"And they leave you in charge of everything while they're traveling. You're a very busy man. I can understand how having to be forced to slow down might go against your better nature. Thanks for painting a broader picture for me."

"What about you, Nurse Westmoreland? What brings you to our quiet little corner of the world? Do you have family here or…?"

"No family. It was a job that I found interesting so I applied. It's a slower pace from the big-city hospital I came from and I like it. And that's my story in a nutshell. Dinner needs my attention and you need to let that pain pill do its work." She didn't look back as she left the room, shutting the door quietly behind her. And that was all she intended for him to know.

Thomas sank back against the pillows for several long moments considering their conversation. As before, he couldn't shake the feeling that there was more about the quiet nurse than she was willing to let on. What did they really know about her? She came highly recommended by Dr. Cuesta, and Thomas knew and trusted his judgment. Was it all as simple as she made it sound? Maybe he'd have a conversation with one of his good friends, the sheriff of Faris County. *Or maybe not.*

Jamie Westmoreland wouldn't be around their lives very long. A week…maybe two. He was always a fast healer. But then again, one never knew about foot injuries. It had to be the pain pill that was making him think such thoughts. The sooner everyone got back to their normal routines, the better. She'd go back to the hospital; he'd get back to the world he knew and controlled. Why did he feel a sudden shadowing of the room around him with those thoughts? Tom closed his eyes and willed for escape from thoughts and feelings.

THE SOUND OF laughter coming from the kitchen area a couple of hours later alerted Thomas to where he might find his son. And the smell of some delicious aroma made his stomach rumble in response. His appetite was definitely coming back after his bout of hospital food. He didn't step into the kitchen right away, preferring to stop and take in the scene inside the room for a moment from his stance in the dining room.

His son was standing on a step stool in front of the broad work counter in the center of the room. He had a kitchen towel around his middle serving as a makeshift apron. His gaze was locked on watching the making of the salad on the cutting board in front of Jamie. She would take one vegetable at a time very patiently, explaining how to clean the item under the faucet in the sink in front of them. She'd hand the item over to Andy and he would do the same maneuvers, tip of tongue locked between his lips in strict concentration, eyes intent on doing as he was told.

He had lettuce, carrots, tomatoes, and finally cucumbers lined up on the drying board. Thomas noted the avid interest that lit his eyes as they watched every move the woman made next to him. Even Pops, seated at the round kitchen table in the corner of the room, coffee cup in hand, watched the progress. Now and then he would nod his approval when Andy shot him a wide grin.

"Do I get to cut these next? Like you can cut them?" Andy asked.

Jamie smiled at him. "I think for the time being, in your novice role—which means you are learning to help the cook—you get to do other things first instead of using knives."

She reached for the lettuce. "We're going to turn over the head of lettuce, like this." She showed Andy how to do it. "Then we pick it up and put a lot of pressure on it by hitting it on the center of the cutting board. That makes this hard center stem core push in, and you'll be able to pull it out. Place both of your hands right on top of mine, and when I count to three, push down as hard as you can. Okay?" Andy followed her directions. She counted and then they pushed. Andy grinned when she turned over the lettuce head and out came the stem, which she allowed him to toss into the trash beside him.

"Now you get to tear the lettuce like this and place it inside the big blue bowl next to you. When we make this type of salad, we want to tear the lettuce instead of chopping or cutting it with a knife. This is the basis for the salad, so it's very important. You get to handle this part." And as Andy followed her directions, she made certain to positively reinforce the job he was doing. Jamie chopped and sliced the other veggies. She asked Andy to put all the other ingredients on top of the lettuce. Then he was allowed to place the lid on the bowl and shake the contents to mix them.

The infinite amount of patience Jamie Westmoreland was exerting with her pupil caught his attention and touched a space in the center of his chest that felt odd. Her instructions were geared to make the lesson both interesting and fun at the same time. He grudgingly had to admit that she was quite good with children, and he wondered if she had experience around them before.

"Well, look who I found standing in the hall watching all the fun?" The voice behind him came from Dottie, who had evidently come in through the living room; he had been too engrossed in watching the scene in front of him to know she was there. Her arrival caught him off guard and he did a quick movement that made him wince as his ankle reminded him that he was still an invalid. When he looked back at the group, he saw the frown creases on Jamie's forehead as she locked on his gaze, her eyes speaking volumes as they moved from his to look pointedly at his foot and then returned with an "I told you so" lift of a fine eyebrow. No words...but she didn't need them. He felt suitably chastised and irritated at the same time.

"Come in and sit down over there with Pops. Can I get you something to drink?" Dottie sat the covered pie carrier down on the counter and spoke the words over her shoulder.

"No, thanks," he managed to say, navigating on the one crutch he had grabbed as he left his pseudo-bedroom earlier. He sat down in the chair Pops had pushed out for him. "We having a party I didn't get an invite to or something?"

"Nope, Dad. But I'm helping Nurse Jamie with supper tonight. She's teaching me how to do cooking. And then I can help Pops, too." The child's voice held the excitement Thomas had already seen in his face.

"I see that. In addition to nursing skills, she has culinary skills, too?" He didn't expect a response and basically let it be known as he turned his attention to Pops. The next few minutes he grilled the man on the latest updates on ranch business while he had been gone. Unfortunately, as much as he would like to admit that he had tuned out other things, he was acutely aware of the movements and lowered conversational tones of the two women and the child across the room.

It was easier to keep his whole brain centered on the topics he knew best when the trio moved from the kitchen into the dining room area after a few minutes. That came to an end when Dottie called to Pops to help him move into the other room.

Pops stood and looked at him. "You heard the woman. We've got our orders."

"People seem to forget I am the one who issues the orders around this ranch." Thomas attempted a semi-teasing tone as he eased himself upright from the chair.

Dottie stood at the doorway, hands on hips, shaking her head at him. "You men sure do waste a lot of air talking nonsense at times. Theodore, we have his chair and foot stool at the end of the table."

"Yes, ma'am." Pops shot Thomas a look as he made the attempt to guide him into the dining room with his hand on his elbow as Thomas limped along beside him on his crutch. It was more or less to quiet any comment he might make on the use of his given name. Ninety-nine percent of the people on the ranch or even the county, knew him simply as Pops. Male, female, kids…he was Pops to all of them. But, from the beginning, Dottie had refused to address him as anything but his given name. If anyone else dared to call him anything other than Pops, he made short work of them. But he made no comment when she did it. It was something that interested Thomas, but he didn't verbalize his thoughts.

"What's this?" Thomas nodded toward the small step stool that had been moved beside the table.

"Nurse Jamie said you had to sit down and put your foot on top of this pillow I put on the stool for you if you were going to sit at the table for dinner," Andy explained.

Thomas's gaze swept the room but there was no sign of the nurse. She had run away and left the child to tell him what to do? *Figures.* He sat down and then noted that three pairs of eyes stayed on him. All of them meant business. Had the woman gained their allegiance, too? It would seem so.

"Please, Dad? Don't you want your foot to get better?"

Andy's voice and the look in those big blue eyes held pure concern. Thomas knew he would fight the other battle later, but his son needed reassurance. He raised his foot and the child helped scoot the stool into place.

Jamie and Dottie had food on the table in the next few minutes. There was the big bowl of fresh salad, green beans with tiny onions and bacon bits, a loaf of warm, fresh bread, and a casserole dish of some mixture of chicken, noodles, and melted cheese on top. There was an apple pie waiting on the sideboard.

Once everyone gathered around the table, Andy took the seat next to Jamie. Thomas nodded at his son. It was always Andy's job to deliver the short blessing of the food. The only difference this time was the postscript he added… *"and please bless Nurse Jamie and make sure she is happy here so she will stay for a long time. Amen."* There were a few beats of silence, and Thomas felt the swift looks at him from Pops and Dottie, and a peek at him from one eye from his son. He also didn't miss the light blush color tinting the aforementioned nurse's cheeks as she concentrated on unfolding her napkin and placing it in her lap.

The food was passed around the table; taking his first bites, Thomas nodded his head. "I have to say, Dottie, that some man needs to snap you up and have this cooking every day in his kitchen. This chicken dish is delicious."

"Well, thank you, Thomas. But I took tonight off. This is all thanks to your Miss Jamie…and her assistant." She added the last with a grin in Andy's direction. "I just brought along a pie. Habits are hard to break, and I always take along something when I go as a guest."

Thomas wasn't certain what stopped him in his tracks faster, the fact that the meal had been prepared not by Dottie, but by Jamie, or the way Dottie had said "your Miss Jamie" and the effect it had on his brain. Both things kept him silent for a few moments. It took Pops clearing his throat as a not-so-subtle reminder to get him back on track. He looked over at Jamie who had her attention on the food in front of her.

"Well, I stand corrected. Thank you, Nurse Jamie, for going above and beyond your duties today. This is a most pleasant surprise."

That brought her gaze to meet his. Then she smiled and nodded. "You all are welcome. I thought it was time to give Dottie a break. And Andy was a very big help in my being able to put this all together. The pie is greatly appreciated and always welcome. It was a team effort."

The rest of the meal passed with light conversation and was an interesting end to a long day. Thomas mused on it later as he leaned against the porch railing, raising a last wave to a departing Dottie. The sun had set and the first evening stars were popping out in profusion across the broad sky. Pops, with Andy and Jasper in his wake, headed toward the horse barn to do a night check.

Jamie turned from her stance at the bottom of the porch

steps where she had bid her goodbye to the woman. "She's really a sweet person. I'm glad I got to meet her."

"She's a hard sell on strangers most times. Guess you passed her litmus test with flying colors. You seem to have bowled over the rest of my ranch in the short time you've been here, too. When people stopped by today, your name was mentioned. And they all had positive comments even after such a short time."

Jamie paused on the top step and glanced up at him. Her face was bathed in the glow of the porch lamps, while his was more in shadows. "That's nice to know. The people I've met here have been very welcoming and helpful."

"And you pause…I wonder if you don't include me in that assessment."

Her gaze was silent and thoughtful on him. There were depths in those chocolate eyes that made him wonder what the layers concealed and how long might it take someone to explore them. Would one ever find all their secrets? "I suppose things can be seen differently depending upon the setting. You could be forgiven for not being on your best behavior when locked up inside a hospital. While here on your ranch and in your environment, one might expect something different."

"Are you saying, Nurse Westmoreland, that I might or might not have improved in your estimation by being here?"

"You aren't up to your full capacity due to your injury. I'm sure there will be changes as you heal and can become your fully active self again."

He couldn't help it. He had to throw back his head and laugh. Then he caught himself. When had something last surprised him so much that he had spontaneously reacted in such a manner? What was it about this woman that made him feel off-kilter and do things that weren't the norm? At least that hadn't been the norm for a very long time...if ever. He stopped and simply allowed his gaze to rest upon the phenomenon beside him.

She returned his silent gaze. Something passed between them. A mercurial, unseen vibration that was felt and unexplainable. A mournful howling of a coyote in the far distance broke the moment, sending her eyes in a frightened race to search out the unseen predator. Thomas felt every one of her nerve endings jump to attention beside him. He straightened his stance into one of immediate protection from some unforeseen menace.

"Relax. It's just a coyote calling out. He's far away and won't come closer. There's no danger."

"There's always danger..." she responded, but not directed at him and spoken just above a whisper. She turned and left him alone on the porch. Had he imagined the words? No, he heard them. Coupled with the look in her eyes that had flashed in a second, it left him questioning again what it was that lay hidden in those eyes. And why in that second had he been moved to want to discover and slay whatever real or imagined dragon that caused her pain? His gaze searched the growing darkness. There were answers out there somewhere. He was determined more than ever to find them.

Chapter Five

"WELL, WELL...LOOK AT you. The lord of the manor rocking the day away on his porch. I better take a photo of this for the gang back at the diner." The tall figure of the county sheriff spoke the words as he stepped from the dust-covered SUV and made his way up the walkway toward the porch, his hand making a playful movement toward his hip.

"Those jokes haven't improved any I see, and you can keep that phone on your belt."

"And your disposition is still as sunny as ever I see, too." The lawman grinned and slid his tall frame into a matching rocker, taking the glass of iced tea his host pushed in his direction. "Thanks for the much-needed cold drink. It might be April on the calendar and was only in the sixties last week, but Mother Nature turned up the heater today for certain." His large swallows took the beverage down to half a glass.

"I'm afraid it's going to be a long, dry summer ahead. Just don't want the fires we had a couple years back. The grass is taking a hell of a lot of water to get it just right for the herds to be moved on them at the end of the month."

Gray Dalton removed his Stetson and settled it on his knee as he crossed his leg, settling into the chair. He pushed up the aviator sunshades to the top of his dark sandy-blond head. Eyes almost a silver-shade of the gray of his name looked over at his host.

"I've known you long enough to know you don't just drop hints about wanting to have me stop by about this time of day. So that tells me that you wanted me here when someone else might not be around. And I can feel a favor coming on a mile away. All okay out here? Any more rustling problems? The family all doing okay on the road?"

"And there we go…" Thomas looked down at the wristwatch with the brown leather strap he wore. "That took you a little longer than I thought it might to bring up 'the family.' And we all know that by *family*, you are really asking about that she-devil sister of mine."

"I have the welfare of all members of your family on my mind. You know that."

"And you know that I know what a load of bull manure that is." Both men grinned at the other.

"My family is busy. My sister, Tori, is being her usually sunny self and giving me heck over letting the fence go down and one of her prized babies wander off to play in a new field. Never mind that I got hurt enough in the process of stopping him that I ended up in the hospital."

"I believe I could hear her yelling at you all the way from Utah. Or was it Wyoming?"

"I have a feeling you know exactly where she is at any given moment…more so than I do. And it's getting to be time for you to be coming up that walk to ask me for her hand in marriage so I can get her off my hands and into yours." Then Thomas frowned. "Maybe that didn't come out exactly as I meant it to, but you get the idea."

"And as you like to say, I believe that is *my* business and no one else's. But it isn't for lack of trying on my part. So we can leave it at that. Now what brings me out here?"

Thomas emptied his tea glass and set it back on the table between them, expelling a long breath. Gray waited.

"While I was in the hospital, I met one of the nurses employed there. She ended up coming out here because the doctor said I would need at-home help…regardless of what I thought."

Gray nodded. "I had heard that."

Thomas shot him a look. "And what else have you and those cowboys around the coffeepot been saying in town?"

"Don't include me in that statement. Being a good lawman, I keep my ears open and mouth shut. But I seem to have heard she is pretty easy on the eyes. And single."

"What else do you know?"

That caused the sheriff to place his glass on the table next. He returned the steady blue gaze from the rancher. "I have no reason to know anything else. Not unless you give me a reason. Is there something I need to be aware of?"

"Not really. It's just that she's staying here, and Andy

seems to have taken quite a liking to her…some sort of puppy-dog worship. I just think it might be wise to know a little more about the person."

"She came recommended by your doctor?"

"Of course she did. And she's good at what she does. It's none of that stuff. Don't you think it wise to find out more about a person staying in my home and being around my child and all that?"

Gray nodded. "I see. I can understand that about being around your child…and I get the 'all' part, too."

It was Thomas's turn to eye the sheriff. "Why do you say that?"

"I think it isn't just for Andy's sake that you want to know more about this particular female. And I am trying to think back as to when it ever happened before in our acquaintance that I sensed such an interest in…"

"Knock it off. Will you do it or not?"

"This might be intriguing. Especially so if that happens to be the lady in question coming from the barn with Andy." He stood from his chair, his gaze on the advancing pair. "I think this might be one of the more interesting aspects of my job." He slid the hat onto his head and the dimpled smile came into view as the pair reached the bottom of the steps. The sheriff didn't wait for introductions from Thomas.

He took the four steps in stride and off came the hat again and his other hand was offered to Jamie. "Hello, I'm Sheriff Gray Dalton, ma'am. I'm an old friend of the

Tremaynes."

"Hello, Sheriff Dalton, it's nice to meet you. I'm Jamie Westmoreland." She placed her hand easily enough into his. Something that Thomas noted with a narrowed gaze. If he didn't know how the man felt about his sister, he might think he was showing a bit too much interest in the nurse. But then again, maybe he was suddenly interested? And maybe his brilliant idea of having Gray do some background work on her past wasn't such a great idea as he originally thought it during his sleepless hours the night before.

"Hi, Uncle Gray. Jamie's really cool. She likes my horse, too. And she even picked up a lizard in the barn. Girls don't like them, but she does."

Gray laughed. "Well, that is indeed a special girl. I am impressed, Miss Westmoreland."

This earned the sheriff a smile from Jamie, which widened into a grin. Not that Thomas was keeping count. "She seems to be the new hero of the ranch in my son's eyes. She is full of surprises."

The words brought all three of them to focus on Thomas. And he might have chosen better words. *Darn female.*

"Well, as much as I would love to stay and have some more tea, I do have crimes to solve."

"Don't let us keep you." Thomas smiled at the man. Their gazes met and much was said between them without a word spoken.

"I'll come by this weekend, and we'll exercise my horse,

okay, Andy?"

"That'll be great!"

"Nice to meet you, Sheriff. And I need to make a call to the hospital, so I'll leave you gentlemen." There went another handshake. He needed to keep a closer eye on Gray Dalton.

"Andy, you need to get busy on your homework. I'll check it over before dinner."

"Yes, sir. Bye, Uncle Gray!"

Thomas and Gray were alone again on the porch.

"She's more than easy on the eyes," Gray noted. "Beautiful lady and you're right… She seems to have the men on this ranch smitten. I would be remiss in my duties if I did not find out more about her."

"You can leave now. Or was that bit about fighting crime just for her sake? Should my sister know about her new competition?"

The hat went back on the head, as he drew the sunglasses in place. "I will do my duty in silence and report anything I find. And your sister probably wouldn't care one way or another. Enjoy the porch…old man." He sent a wave over his retreating back along with a laugh. Then he was gone in a haze of dust.

"THE SHERIFF SEEMS to be a very nice person," Jamie

commented in response to Andy's unending monologue at the dinner table later that evening. He extolled the many virtues of the lawman.

"He and my sister have known each other a long time. Whenever she settles long enough, he'll probably put the noose around his neck and pop the question. He's mooned after her as long as any of us can remember." Jamie's gaze met the rancher's across the table. Since it was just the three of them for dinner, they were eating the meal in the kitchen at the smaller dining table. Just a typical evening meal for a small family.

Right.

The minute the thought crossed her mind, she chased it away with sarcasm. The man seated across from her no more wanted her there than she wanted to be there. Somehow they were managing to be civil to each other. If for no other reason than Andy's presence.

"You don't seem to be in favor of matrimony?"

He cocked his head to the side and considered the question. "Let's say I'm in favor of it for other people who don't know better."

"I see. I take it you are in favor of the sheriff joining your family?"

"If that's what my sister wants, then my brothers and I are ready for it to get done."

She returned her gaze to the plate in front of her, tamping down her reaction to his remarks. But he evidently noticed.

"Don't tell me you're one of those bleeding-heart romantics who secretly have a stash of those novels in her closet, are you? Somehow I would have expected better."

She set her fork down on the edge of her plate, then reached for her tea glass, taking a sip before returning it to its place. Then she looked up at the man waiting for her response. He was clearly baiting her.

"I have a very strenuous job at times. I enjoy a good book as well as the next person in order to escape reality if only for a couple of hours. And yes, I read romances. I also read biographies, travel books, comedies, and more."

"No mysteries? True crime whodunits?"

She eyed him steadily, not acknowledging the jump in her heart rate. "No. I don't care for that genre. And Andy..." She turned her attention to the child who had been studiously pushing the vegetables around his plate. "If you have any hopes of having the peppermint ice cream for dessert, I think your father will say that at least half of those peas and carrots need to disappear...inside you." She looked at the man for his input.

"Right. Eat your vegetables, little man. Nurse Jamie intends to keep us *all* healthy while she's here."

"Yes, sir. Yes, ma'am, Nurse Jamie. The peas are okay, but the little carrots not so much. I'll hold my breath and that way I won't taste them." He proceeded to do just that.

Jamie couldn't hide her smile. How often had she used

the same trick when faced with something she didn't want to eat? That brought another thought from her past and the smile faded. She stood, brushing it aside. Gathering her plate and glass, she moved to the cabinet. She heard a chair scrape behind her, and then Thomas set his emptied plate and glass next to hers.

"I cleaned my plate, so that means I get dessert, right?"

Jamie looked up at the man standing next to her. And registered just how blue those eyes could be when taken up close. They were returning her perusal with one of their own. There was a half smile that was captured by the deep grooves that framed the mouth. Both of them seemed just as surprised and caught off-guard in the same moment. There was a long pause.

Jamie's brain was trying to get back on track. It was sparking back to life enough for her to respond. "Dessert?"

"Ice cream. Unless you have a better idea?" The words were low enough that no one else could hear them. She thought, amid the sudden flutter inside her stomach.

"Can we have cookies, too?" That small high-pitched voice was strong enough to shatter the moment. Jamie turned back to the sink, gasping for air and sanity at the same time. "That's a question for your father. I need to run up to my room for a moment. Then I'll come back and take care of the dishes." She didn't wait for any response. At least she didn't run from the kitchen but managed to walk sedately into the next room. Then she ran up the stairs.

She only stopped when she was inside her room, leaning with her back against the closed door. *Are you crazy?* Was she? What was that in the kitchen? Was the man playing with her? She had men flirt with her before. She wasn't a prude. And Thomas Tremayne was a very good-looking male. If you liked tall, dark, gorgeous eyes, broad shoulders, and all the other attributes she had done her best to ignore over the past two weeks being around him at the hospital and in his home. But she was there to work. *Period.* Their worlds were vastly different.

And she would be gone in another week. She was certain she would never see the man again. He had let his feelings be known about certain things that they differed upon. What would he have said if she had said the words that came to mind when he asked about reading? How would a man like him ever understand that those books he made fun of had actually saved her on many a lonely, fright-filled night? They had opened up a fantasy world where her reality was far removed. They helped her survive. She wouldn't shy away from the truth about reading romance novels… She just didn't explain the truth of why.

And she wondered then, what would have been his response if she had said that no, she didn't read whodunits or crime novels because she didn't need to. She had lived out one in real life…and barely survived only by her own wits. She'd lost her parent in the final chapter. Closing her eyes, she drew up her mother's face from the past. It was blurry, her face fading away. That was good…wasn't it? But then, if she faded away completely, Jamie would be left really alone with nothing but the bad stuff.

She had tried to remember what a smiling face her mother once had, but she couldn't. Because she couldn't remember a moment when that had ever been the case for her mother. And especially not in those final days. The knocking of the door behind her jarred her back to the present and sent the past back into the box in her mind where she fought to keep it.

Opening the door, she found Andy standing before her. He raised his hands toward her, and she saw the three cookies lying in the center of a napkin. "Dad said you might want these for later. And I helped him, and we did the dishes in the kitchen and you don't have to do anything. He said tomorrow we could show you the big bulls if you want to go with us after breakfast."

Big bulls? That didn't sound like Thomas was following the "take it easy" plan at all. Darn right she'd be there to either stop him or try to keep him from doing more harm to his injury. The man was a law unto himself. And stubborn to no end.

"Thank you for the cookies and for taking care of the dishes. I will certainly go with you to see these big bulls you talk so much about."

The grin split his face from one corner to the other. "Awesome! I'll tell Dad. It'll be a lot of fun!"

Chapter Six

*I*T'LL BE A *lot of fun.* Why did those words echo through her mind as she stood in mud that was just less than the consistency of glue, wishing she had a bandanna to cover her nose from the less than aromatic stench? The herd in the enclosed area left a lot to be desired in opening up a person's sinuses.

"Enjoying yourself?" The question came from the tall rancher who was in his element, complete with full cowboy gear and chaps of brown leather and fringe trim with the ranch's brand stitched on one leg. The crutch was the only jarring item in the picture. At least he hadn't been able to ditch it under her eagle eye.

"People seem to be very concerned that I should derive enjoyment out of this experience." Her reply brought a raised eyebrow. "I will admit that I had no idea that cattle could get to be this size. These animals are huge, and they are your pride and joy."

He shook his head. "Nope. Not *mine.* This herd is part of the culmination of the insanity my little sister has infected her brain with over the last few years. From the time she was barely able to saddle her own horse, she has been enthralled with building a herd of the biggest, baddest bucking bulls to be found anyplace in this country. And she's managed to do it, too. But this is not my idea, and she'd set you straight soon enough if she heard that." He finished with a soft chuckle at the thought.

"Well, I think she might also have something to say about this pair of boots of hers you forced me to wear today. Don't get me wrong… They've come in handy given where we've been walking and all, but I doubt they'll ever be the same."

That morning, after a quick breakfast, she had stepped out onto the porch to be met by Thomas, who shoved a pair of brown leather boots into her hands. "I think these will do. You seem to be about my sister's size. You best wear them and save those prissy tennis shoes of yours." He had headed toward the pickup without allowing time for her to tell him what she thought of the idea.

Luckily, they fit. And her "prissy" shoes were still white and waiting back at the ranch.

"You're welcome, Nurse Jamie. I know you didn't pack for a working ranch. And I was right given those scrubs you seem to like so much."

"They *are* part of my job. I did wear jeans today in honor of this trip to see the big, bad bulls. Does this trip have a purpose other than to look at cows?"

The laugh that came from deep within him caught her

off guard. It was both spontaneous and not unpleasant. Again, he surprised her. But she still didn't care for being the object of any joke.

"Okay, forgive me. Don't get that scowl on your face." He tamped down the laugh. "I would have thought that you being a nurse and all…and knowing the difference in males and females, you might realize that you wouldn't call these animals 'cows.' Bulls are male with all the appropriate male parts…as you can see from these in front of you. And cows are females with all…"

"I get it." She cut him off. "Pardon me for the slip of the tongue. I promise to stand here quietly and bask in the magnificence of the males before me and their awesome attributes."

Were his shoulders shaking again? His face was half-turned from her, but when he faced her, it was plain he could barely contain himself with his next statement.

"Awesome attributes. And are you referring to *all* the males within your eyesight right now?"

Jamie looked at the man. What was he…? And then she saw the dancing gleam of a jokester in the blue depths. He had her. Or did he?

"You have an appointment this afternoon for your foot X-ray. We need to get moving." She turned away and then stopped. Jamie gave him a parting shot over her shoulder. "Perhaps we can use the X-ray machine to also help answer your question for you. It can locate even the minutest of things." She had effectively silenced him by the look of stunned surprise on his face. She continued to the pickup, a lightness returning to her steps for some reason. *Take that, you arrogant cowboy.*

SILENCE FILLED THE truck on the way back to the ranch. Even Andy had quieted down, and there were a few yawns from the back seat. Once back at the house, they had changed clothes and Andy was given over to Pop's watchful gaze, much to the child's disappointment. It was only Jamie and the patient headed into town for his appointment.

Thomas had to hand it to the woman beside him. She sat so prim and proper in her hospital scrubs, her hair caught back in the sleek ponytail. Very *efficient*. He caught himself more than once wondering what her hair would look like set free. She had moments when the mask slipped, and he saw a different side of what was turning out to be a multi-faceted woman. He had pushed her buttons…most often on purpose. He had pushed the limits of most people's patience with his sliding along the edge of the envelope in following her medical directives. Each time, she had simply given him that "look" that reminded him of those his mother once gave him…many times, actually, over the years. The woman would bide her time and then make her point known. And he had really pushed Jamie today at the bull pens. *Why?* Had he wanted to see how far he could go? Maybe he wanted to shake up that coolly poised demeanor of hers. *Why?* Each time he thought he had figured out an answer to those whys…he pushed it away and refused it.

Jamie Westmoreland was there for a short time. To do her job. Then she would leave. And that is when he realized in the last couple of days that thought didn't sit well…not like it first did. When was the last time a female had stood her ground with him? Gone toe to toe with him? Made him question some of his choices? A woman who wasn't his sassy little sister? *None.*

What would it take to find the real woman beneath the layers she used to throw people off track? And then that thought usually led to his thinking back on his life to date. Had he let one bad experience with a woman color all the rest? It had been a pretty awful time…having the floor jerked out from beneath him while he had an infant depending on him for his very life and he was just a cowboy faced with being two parents in one. Not to mention the fact he felt like the world's biggest fool for being tricked by a heartless blonde in a pair of tight jeans and a sexy smile who had only wanted one thing…his bank account.

So maybe he had gone off track the other way…too much burying desires and wants in bad memories. But he hadn't found any female that caught his eye, let alone challenged him and kept him off-center with a look, a flash of a smile, a pair of doe eyes that made him think all sorts of pleasurable and downright sinful things with just a glance. If he wasn't careful, he might just lose his grip on reality. But would that be so awful? What if he took a chance? Those thoughts filled his mind and kept him quiet on the ride to town.

They were on the outskirts of Faris when she spoke across the silence. "I saw where Tori lives as we drove by it earlier, and I caught a glimpse of your aunt Sal's home. You said that Truitt and Trey live there also when they're not on the rodeo circuit?"

"That's correct. Aunt Sallie moved into the main house when our parents died. She's an artist and planning to open her own art gallery in town in the next year or so. But Trey isn't around all that much. Truitt is building onto his horse herds. When he can find a way to get off the circuit, he would prefer to stay with his own company and be just as satisfied training roping horses and such."

Once they pulled into the parking lot, Jamie was out of the truck before the engine died. He quickly grabbed his hat, shoving it on his head as he made a grab for the crutch. She was standing on the sidewalk watching his approach.

"Where's the fire? You don't give a guy enough time to even open the door for you."

"Do I need help with the door? This isn't a date. And if you had allowed me to drive you today, then we wouldn't have to be standing here having such a discussion. Come on, we don't want to be late for the appointment." She turned and left him to follow…or not. He had half a mind to do just that. Not follow. But then a wiser voice told him that might not be a good idea.

Choose your battles, son. His father had given him that advice on more than one occasion. It seemed most appropriate for that moment.

"You disappeared." He came through the door after the X-ray tech and found Jamie just walking into the outer office.

"You're a big boy. I didn't think you needed me holding your hand for you. Or did you?"

"No, I did not need you to do that." He slid his hat onto his head. Then he smiled at her. "But I thought you might have wanted to check out the other X-ray."

Before she could think, she spoke. "What other X-ray? Is there a problem?" She looked to where the tech had been standing, but he had left them.

"No problem. Everything checks out just fine. Some things bigger and better than others." He winked and flashed a cheeky grin.

She felt the heat rising up the back of her neck. He was not going to have the satisfaction of getting a blush out of her. The game of words was done. She headed toward the door, leaving him to close it behind them.

"So, is there a fire?" he asked again.

"No fire. We need to stop by the pharmacy and pick up the refill on one of your meds. Then we can head back."

This time, he managed to get a couple of steps ahead of her when she was detained by one of the staff who stopped them at the front door to say hello to her. Thomas opened the passenger door with a flourish as she stepped off the curb.

What was he up to? Trying to stay one step ahead of the man was wearing her energy level down. She stepped up into the truck and he shut the door. He smiled. And it was a sight to see as evidenced by the way her pulse was suddenly tap dancing. It made matters worse when he leaned into the open window. "And no…this isn't a date. *This* time."

Two words. *This time.* What was he doing? Had he just given notice there would be a next time and it *would* be a date? There went that unfamiliar flutter in the center of her body.

As he pulled away from the curb, he turned the vehicle in the opposite direction of the pharmacy. She looked at him. "Are we taking a new route to the pharmacy I don't know about?"

"I'm hungry. I think we have time to stop by the diner and grab a late lunch. I know how meticulous you are about your patient's meal schedule. I'm just following your orders."

She shook her head. "Funny how you pick and choose when you follow my orders."

That just brought another of those surprising smiles in

her direction. Would he stop doing that? It was definitely something that threw her off her concentration on keeping things strictly professional. Did he do it on purpose? She didn't like the feeling that came along with that question. It had taken her a long time and much therapy to get to where she no longer looked at every male as a potential threat. But Thomas Tremayne was a totally different entity. He made her feel things she had only read about. And she couldn't shake the feeling that there was the potential for danger ahead. The sort of danger that could easily break a heart.

"Are you okay? You look a little pale all of a sudden." His gaze held concern. Jamie summoned a small smile and shook her head.

"No problem. I should have taken more time to eat a better breakfast this morning. Lunch is a good idea."

And it turned out to be a good idea. She had to admit that. The diner was quiet—after lunch was done and dinner was yet to be on people's minds. And the other pleasant surprise was the fact that Thomas seemed determined to be on his best behavior. Conversation had begun easily, and they maintained it over the burgers and fries. If he ventured into personal questions, she was able to move it back to questions about the ranching business and his siblings.

"Truitt is the next brother in line. He's the brains of the group. He's quiet, but he's got a quick wit and he is a genius with business planning. Right now, he's with the team where he does book work, but also dons clown makeup and becomes a totally different person. He's one great bullfighter."

"Bullfighter? You fight the bulls you raise? I think I'm lost."

He didn't make fun of her question or laugh it off. Thomas smiled and explained. "In rodeo, when bull riding begins, you used to have guys come out dressed in some crazy getups, clown makeup, you name it. Well, that has evolved as rodeo has evolved. They still dress a bit comical, but don't let that fool you. They are athletes, not clowns. They have one function and that is to save a cowboy in trouble. They put themselves between the downed rider and a very mad bull. Truitt is a real hero in my book...in more ways than one."

She sensed there was more to what he said. She waited for him to continue if he chose to do so.

"I don't know how much you know about our family and the tragedy we had a few years back." The words came out slowly, but in a matter-of-fact telling.

"I'm afraid I don't know all that much."

"You'll hear about it sooner or later so you might as well hear it right. Our entire family was in a bad accident. We were headed home from town. It had been storming up in the canyons. We came upon a crossing and the bridge had given out. We were sitting there about to turn around when a truck came along...too fast. It couldn't stop in time. It hit us and pushed our vehicle into the flood waters. Some of us were able to get out. Some were not. My father and mother, my youngest brother Tyler, and Truitt's fiancé Skylar didn't make it out alive. Truitt was badly hurt and basically clung to a tree overnight until he made his way to a farmhouse and got help. He was torn up physically. And emotionally…well, it took a toll. He hides his pain and is pretty much a loner. Except in the arena, and then he is a different person beneath the makeup."

"I'm so very sorry about your family. I had no idea." If he had chosen not to continue after that, she would have understood. But it seemed once he began, he didn't want to stop. So she sat and listened.

"Then there's Trey; he's the wild man of the group. He's the bronc riding champion and heartbreaking rodeo cowboy, the favorite of the ladies. Things seem to come easily to the guy, and he's after another gold belt buckle. He's got quite a collection already. Who knows when or if he'll ever settle down. He's a good guy, but he seems to be trying to prove something that none of us can quite understand. Footloose and fancy free is his style."

"And then there's your little sister?"

"And then there's Victoria. But don't call her that. She is Tori. She is obstinate, hardheaded, full of sass, and cries over animals and sad movies. But I didn't tell you that part."

"And the sheriff is crazy about her. But does she feel the same?"

There was a shrug. "I've given up trying to figure that

one out. I think Gray is in it to the end. But Tori…she is so driven to have that number one bull at Nationals. She's out to prove something… I guess that's the best way to put it. And she doesn't share what she thinks about Gray with her brothers. I might have mentioned once before how much you two might have in common."

He stopped, but she wasn't going to let him off the hook that easy. "Yes, I got the message. But what would they say about the oldest Tremayne brother? Who is he?"

Her question clearly took him by surprise. She was afraid he was going to take the easy way out and shrug it off. But Thomas didn't. After a few moments, he spoke again.

"Thomas Tremayne, Junior. Father of Thomas Tremayne, the third. He's a man who takes duty and responsibility very seriously…perhaps too much so at times. At least that's what the majority seem to agree upon. I married young, and my wife was a big mistake in my life. She decided to leave when Andy was three months old.

"At least I used to say it was a huge mistake. But one day my little sister pointed out to me a black-and-white fact. Without my ex, I wouldn't have Andy in my life right now. In my early days on the rodeo circuit with my dad, we were team ropers…and I was the typical stud cowboy who enjoyed the adoration of my share of buckle bunnies." He stopped to explain. "A buckle bunny is the term for a female rodeo fan that wants to collect the shiny belt buckle of a champion…if only for a night. If you get the drift."

"I get the drift. I've heard the term before. Continue."

"One of those young females was Casey, who looked great in a pair of jeans and made me think she was in it for all the right reasons. I ignored the warnings of my siblings. And she came up pregnant and I did the right thing. The only problem was she didn't want any part of being a stay-at-home wife and mother. That was a little too real for her. So she took a lot of money and she left. A couple of years later, she was killed in a plane crash. And there's not much more to say about the ensuing years. I did what I had to do to keep the ranch paying the bills and my son getting what he needed to grow up. And that's the story of Thomas."

"You quit rodeo? To stay on the ranch and raise your son? I'd say there's a lot more to having been successful at that than what you just shared. Andy is an amazing little boy."

He nodded his agreement. "Thank you. It's taken an entire ranch full of people to help me raise him. But I think you have heard enough of the Tremaynes for one sitting. Let's go." Thomas reached for the check, laid some bills on top of it on the table, and guided her across the diner toward the front door.

Jamie had quite a bit of information to digest about the family…and about what formed the man beside her. It kept her mind occupied as they made the pharmacy stop and headed out of town. She was brought out of her reverie as the truck jostled over a metal cattle guard as they left the main road.

"Is this a shortcut to the ranch?"

"Nope. I thought I'd show you the favorite place of the Tremaynes and why we love this land so much…one of its hidden treasures."

She was intrigued.

Tall trees cast shade over the one-lane roadway. New green grass was visible in openings where she could see pastures mixed with the landscape. Topping a hill, the truck took a couple more turns down the other side and came to a halt. In front of them was a huge expanse of water…the blue of which reminded her of a certain cowboy's eyes. That made her smile. Tall cypress trees rimmed the area, the gnarled roots twisting and twining their way along the banks of an expanse of river that flowed steady and then cascaded over rocks that formed natural dams and rapids.

"Let's get out." He left his hat on the dashboard and his crutch in the back seat. The nurse in her noted the fact, and she hurried to lend him an arm if needed.

"Don't worry, Nurse Jamie," he said, a smile noting her medical bearing. "I promise to not fall flat on my face in front of you."

"Humor me."

He looked at her offered arm and considered things for a moment. "You might have a better idea there."

Right. Better idea? With his arm looped around hers…or was it vice versa? Why wasn't her mind as clear as it normally would be? She tried to concentrate on the semi-rough pathway that had been carved out over the years by many visitors before them. They made it to the riverbank, and she took in the site.

"You were right. This is a real treasure. I can imagine how often you and your brothers and sister must have come here. The water is so blue and so clear."

"We still do. And once in a while, we'll have a barbecue down here…maybe invite some friends to come over. Most often, each of us will come down here when we just need to have some peace in our life or close our eyes and float on our backs as we think through some problem or such. But it's all good memories here. And now you know one of our secrets."

"Secrets? There're more? Any you care to share?" She was teasing. But then she made the mistake of meeting his gaze. There was something there she couldn't read. It was strange, new, primitive, and yet full of promises. It picked up her heart and flipped it like a pancake. Thomas didn't reply…not with words.

It was as if it was meant to be… There was no other way the moment was going to play out. Everything that came before had brought them to this spot and this moment…and this kiss.

Lips, strong and sure and warm, claimed hers. A tremble went through her from head to toe and then back. An arm drew her up to his side, a palm sliding upward along her chin to cup it in a gentle caress. Her free hand splayed itself on the center of his strong chest, and the steady beats of his heart beneath her fingers increased in speed as his kiss deepened. She felt more alive in those few moments than she had felt in a very long time. Something fell away from her senses, and they reveled in the feel of a strange new sensation of freedom. Her lips responded to his, and when his stilled for a moment and loosened their hold on hers, it was her lips that sought his out and brought him back where he belonged. To where she needed him.

There was a leashed need within him. It was answered by the same desire within her. They fed off each other, drank as if they could not get enough. It was he who finally lifted his head and took in a deep, calming breath. A matching shudder resounded through her body.

"And that's another secret I'll share with you. But don't expect me to apologize for overstepping the patient and nurse boundary. I'm not one bit sorry if some rule was broken. Just know Nurse Jamie Westmoreland that I intend to kiss you again, and most certainly when this patient and nurse nonsense is done. We best leave now while I can keep that promise in its G-rated form."

Chapter Seven

THE SILENCE INSIDE the pickup was so thick that a chain saw might be needed to cut it. At least that's how it felt to Jamie as she wished the earth would just swallow her up. The kiss had to be her worst regret ever. How could she have behaved like some love-starved teenager? What must he think from her response? She knew better. She was supposed to be a professional. He was her patient…nothing more, nothing less. And by his protracted silence, he was probably thinking much the same thing…regretting it had happened at all. They both just got carried away in the moment. That's what it was. *Wasn't it?*

Luck was with Jamie as they pulled into the driveway of the ranch house a few minutes later. She had dreaded the evening ahead trying to pretend that all was well and the trip to town had been uneventful. The thought of making small talk with the man who had kissed her senseless one moment and then maintained a stony silence all the way back to the ranch afterward was knotting her insides.

The sight of Dottie's SUV brought a silent sigh of reprieve. She didn't hesitate once the engine was turned off.

And Jamie didn't wait for her patient as she normally would have. With a smile on her face, she stepped into the hallway to greet the visitor. With luck, she could avoid the man of the house the rest of the evening.

"We'll have the crew load out. That way, we'll be able to hop the plane and be at the ranch in time for the main event. You've got the box still hidden away in the tack room, right?"

"Yes, Truitt, the box is right where you left it. Pops will have everything lined out just like you told him a half dozen times, and how Trey told him the three times he called, and how Tori amplified during her last text."

There was a low half-chuckle, half-grunt over the phone. It was about the sum total of any mirth that his sibling displayed. But Truitt had always had a soft spot for his nephew Andy. For that reason, Thomas was grateful and would nod his head and listen to yet another reminder.

"Well, he's been waiting a long time for this birthday to come around. A guy only turns seven once." Then there was silence, and Thomas knew that the same thought had followed his words on both sides of the call. Their youngest brother had just turned seven when they lost him. And as each of the remaining siblings had learned early on, they shut the door on the rest of the memories that came along with that tragic day in their lives. Truitt cleared his throat, and his voice returned to its deep rumble.

"I've got to go find your brother and rescue him from whatever female caught his attention after the last go-around. He needs to get his mind in the game. Jett Tyson is just ten points away heading into the next ride."

Thomas ran a quick hand through his hair and with a snort of disgust added, "Trey needs some sense kicked into his head. Maybe the fall would do him some good. Us talking to him over and over rolls off his back like water off a duck. Just be careful coming home and we'll see you all when you get here." The call was done.

Sliding his hat down on his forehead, Thomas grabbed the crutch as much out of habit as anything. The X-ray had pleased the doctors, but they gave him another week to "take it easy" before he could toss the hindering piece of metal. He had to admit that he needed to rest it more and maybe he had trashed some pain pills when he shouldn't have. That thought brought another one to the forefront of his brain. Another "problem" as it were. Only this one was a human problem and one he had no idea how to make go away.

He had created the problem. Kissing Jamie three days ago at the swimming hole was just as fresh as if it happened a moment ago. The taste of her lips, the feel of her body curving into his, and the smell of her faint scent of perfume still lingered where he didn't want it to. It would be one thing if he could mark it up to being without the company of a female for a little while. But his brain shot that full of holes. It wasn't just *any* female…it was this one. Jamie Westmoreland had walked right up to him and knocked his idea of keeping things on an impersonal, strictly business basis on its backside. And it had been his natural need to self-protect that had caused the friction between them.

For the first time, he felt unsure. Exactly of what he was uncertain, he had no definite idea. It was a general feeling of being off keel…especially where she was concerned. She had such compassion for those around her…with the possible exception of him. The way she had responded to Andy and how he did the same with her both pleased him and set off warnings. What if his son got too attached to her? She would leave them one day…and soon? Without a backward glance or thought? And then he'd be left to mend his son's heart. But what about *his*?

And that two-by-four smacked him upside the head. Where did that come from? Why should he be concerned about *his* heart? It was just a kiss for heaven's sake. And yet, even as he said those words to himself, there was a louder voice overriding it all. Maybe the impossible had snuck up on him and trapped him before he knew it? He had fancied himself head over heels about a woman once before and his judgment had been proven very wrong. But Jamie wasn't Casey, not by any stretch of the imagination. And that was dangerous. Jamie didn't strike him as a woman who would be giving her heart to anyone…at least not without good cause. That man would have to have a tough hide and a heck of a lot of stamina. But then, she just might be worth it all. That made him shake his head and stamp his good foot. He needed to get moving and clear his head of a doe-eyed female.

"Do you like the drawing of the horse? I think he needs some work." Andy had come running down the sidewalk and climbed into the rear passenger seat, handing over a paper to Jamie with excitement in his voice.

Jamie grinned and took the paper, studying it while the little boy buckled his seat belt and deposited his backpack on the floorboard in front of him. "I think this is very good, Andy. And anything gets better with more practice, so if you're not happy with this one, you can do another until you're pleased. But I really like this one. It reminds me of your horse. It has beautiful eyes."

"And it's yours. I drew it for you. If you really like it, you can have it."

There was that zing inside her chest again. Andy had an uncanny ability to catch her off-guard and do something that she knew would make it very hard to not be around him any longer. That shadow always came along and brought her back to reality. Her time was growing shorter by the day. In the beginning, she had wanted it done before it began. Now, she didn't want to count the number of days remaining as they were growing much too short.

Pulling away from the curb, she concentrated on other things. "How about we stop at the drive-thru at the Snow Cone Factory? I think you worked hard this week in school and deserve something special."

He couldn't nod fast enough. "Yes, ma'am! I sure could use one of those strawberry and banana ones with extra sprinkles on the top. Could we get one of those?"

"I think that would be a good idea."

Andy began a rundown of how his Friday had gone. Jamie listened with a smile on her face. What would it be like to have a little boy like him as her own? Despite trying not to do so, she hadn't been able to keep Andy from getting past her defenses and staking a claim on a piece of her heart. That was because he was a combination of a child and a little man. He was more mature than most of his peers at the same age. But she shouldn't be surprised. The grown-ups around him had brought him right into their daily world, and he had followed happily.

She had to admit that a lot of it had to do with his father. Thomas Tremayne loved his son beyond measure... No one could fault him for that. And anyone would be hard put to fault him in any way, shape, or form for the things he did to provide for Andy; always placing his well-being first and foremost. The people around this child had an immense amount of love and caring, and Andy was indeed blessed.

Still, Jamie couldn't help but wish he had the one adult figure he had done without…a mother. It was clear to her that Andy had become fascinated and then fixated on some storyline where she would stay and fill that role. That was where she worked hard to always remember and not cross that finite line in the sand that would only bring heartache if crossed.

It was a fine line she walked to not encourage that thinking. Her world was much different from Andy's and the rest of the Tremaynes'. They had roots that went back a century or more on this land. She had never lived in one place longer than a couple of years, until she had grown up and earned enough to support herself. She could count her friends on one hand…and there was no family…no blood family that was. The shadow that hovered in that box at the back of her mind threatened to spoil the afternoon, and she shook her head. Those thoughts were forbidden. She and Andy had a date with the snow cone man as Andy liked to call the older gentleman who always had a smile and something to say that brought a laugh or at least a big grin from his customers.

Andy skipped ahead of her as they left the SUV and headed toward the doorway. Just as they got to that door, it opened, and a tall figure grinned at them. "Come in, come in. Don't tell me that Andy Tremayne has been behaving enough to have a snow cone this afternoon?"

"I sure have behaved. Nurse Jamie says so. And I get my favorite flavor with sprinkles, too." He headed toward the counter. Jamie smiled at the man beside her. "Good afternoon, Sheriff Dalton. Yes, I can verify the fact that Andy has worked very hard this week in school and done his chores at the ranch, so he gets a reward."

"Gray, please. We aren't all that formal around here." He walked beside her to the glass-fronted display cases.

"Gray," she said with a smile in return. "I take it that you felt a reward for yourself was necessary this afternoon?" She nodded at the remains of the cup in his hand. "And please call me Jamie."

"Yes, Jamie, I felt it was a perfect afternoon for a treat. We know what Andy is going to choose, but what about you?"

"I just like plain strawberry...no crème or sprinkles or any of the other toppings. I guess I'm dull that way."

"I doubt anyone could call you dull. You are a lady who knows her mind, and that's the way it is."

Their orders were placed, and Jamie found it was a losing battle to argue with the lawman when it came time to pay at the register. "It's an overdue welcome gift to our town from me." They both laughed.

"This looks like quite a little party going on here."

"Hi, Dad! I got a reward for doing good this week. And my party is tomorrow." Andy was the first to respond to the sudden appearance of Thomas inside the shop.

Jamie noted that while he might have a half smile on his face, it didn't quite reach his eyes. Did it bother him that she had stopped to treat his son to his favorite snow cone? She couldn't think why it should.

"I see. And you were invited, too." Thomas's gaze was on the lawman, who was looking like he was enjoying some secret joke that she had no idea about. He shook his head.

"I was just lucky enough to be in the right place at the right time. Jamie and Andy came in as I was about to leave. I decided I had earned a reward, too, and could stay and enjoy their company. Too bad you came late."

"My misfortune. But it looks like Andy and *Jamie* were well-entertained with you."

Jamie saw the sharpened look Thomas added just for his friend's benefit. And it clicked. Was he upset with them? Why? And then another thought hit her, and she almost choked at the sheer laughable nature of it. Thomas Tremayne couldn't be upset because she was enjoying Gray Dalton's company, could he? That would be borderline jealousy. And the thought sobered her. She had never had anyone actually be jealous over her…not that she knew of at any rate. It was a strange feeling…slightly giddy. But why? He couldn't be interested in her, not like that. Right? Had the kiss they shared meant something more to him than she could have believed? That in itself was sobering.

"Tori will be home in time for the party. In case you haven't had time to call her."

Gray simply nodded his head. "Thanks for the information. I assumed I'd see her at the birthday party. Looks to be quite a celebration for some special person."

"For me!" The child left his snow cone long enough to speak up. "I'm going to be seven."

"I seem to have heard that rumor a time or two." Gray grinned at the child. "And in order for me to be there for your shindig, I better get back to my office and work on a stack of paperwork waiting for me."

"I'm sorry we kept you from—" Jamie didn't get to finish.

"I'm not, and it was a very pleasant way to spend a bit of my afternoon. You can steal me away for a snow cone rendezvous anytime, *Jamie*." If Jamie didn't know better, she might have taken that smile he bestowed upon her with that quick wink as pure flirtation. But she knew he had his sights set on Tori Tremayne. At least that was what Thomas had told her.

"Don't let us keep you, Sheriff. I'm sure we'll see you tomorrow afternoon." Thomas actually opened the door for the man. And then he looked expectantly at her.

She turned toward Andy. "Done? Good, then take another napkin and go over your chin there." She pointed to a spot he had missed. "Now, we can leave."

Jamie didn't spare the man another glance. Instead, she concentrated on getting Andy settled into his spot in the SUV, and then rounded the vehicle to her door. Only Thomas was there and opened the door for her. She stepped to the door but didn't get in right away. Lowering her voice so the pair of big ears in the back seat wouldn't hear, she met the rancher's gaze head-on.

"The sheriff was very nice to both Andy and me. Whatever put a burr under your saddle needs to be dealt with. But you were rude to your friend and embarrassed me. All I tried to do was give Andy a special treat for his good week in school. Luckily, at least he still enjoyed it in spite of your bad manners." She slid behind the wheel and closed her door with a solid thud. Jamie did not glance back at the man she left standing in the parking lot.

Chapter Eight

IT MIGHT AS well been Christmas morning given the level of expectancy and excitement exhibited by Andy. He woke with the sunrise, was out to do his chores, and got back to the kitchen for the breakfast that featured his requested favorite breakfast tacos. Jasper was in his spot under his chair to take care of any morsels that might "accidentally" fall onto the floor.

"Can someone tell me why my calendar has a big red circle around today's date? I can't imagine what that could mean." The voice came from the tall figure standing just inside the back doorway. His gaze was on the child who suddenly left his chair and was lifted easily into a pair of arms as if he weighed no more than a feather. The pair shared a hug, and the man grinned at Andy's enthusiasm.

"Uncle Truitt! You know it's my birthday today. I circled your calendar for you so you wouldn't forget."

"As if that would be possible." Then the man looked over to where Jamie was standing with a smile on her face at the pair. He paused and waited.

She stepped forward, set the plate of tacos on the table,

and then looked up at the man. "You must be the famous Uncle Truitt I've heard so much about from Andy. You had a long trip back here. Would you like some of these breakfast tacos and a cup of coffee?"

She received a nod. "Thanks, ma'am, they do smell good."

Andy returned to his chair and his uncle moved forward. He slid his hat off his head and placed it on a peg beside the door. Jamie set a freshly poured coffee cup on the table. Then she held out her hand to him and waited.

"I'm Jamie Westmoreland. I'm here on a nursing assignment for your brother."

He accepted the handshake. "I might have heard something about that from Tori and this young'un in a text or two…or three." He took a sip of the coffee. Jamie settled into a chair across from him.

"I understand that you're involved with the rodeos as a bullfighter. I have to say I don't know if you're very brave or maybe short a few marbles."

The man almost choked on the drink he was taking as she spoke. He looked over at her, searching her gaze as it stayed level on him.

"That's fair enough. You do speak your mind." He paused. Then he nodded. "I appreciate that."

"And Nurse Jamie gains another admirer." This came from Thomas as he entered the room, evidently hearing the last exchange as he crossed into the kitchen. He helped himself to some coffee but declined to take a seat, instead leaning against the cabinet behind him.

Jamie did not react nor look in his direction. She helped herself to one of the tacos from the platter and began to eat.

"Everyone likes Nurse Jamie. She's even cool around lizards and stuff," Andy stated.

"Impressive. I can see that she is special." Truitt's gaze was leveled not on the child but on his brother.

"Well, *I* can see that daylight is burning and we have a lot to do if we're having a party here this afternoon. You done? I could use another pair of hands with the firewood Pops called about for the pits."

Truitt took another sip of coffee as he stood from the chair. "Thanks for the breakfast, ma'am. It hit the spot."

"You're welcome, Truitt. And please, call me Jamie."

He nodded and reached for his hat. He shot a look at his brother. "Well, are you coming or too busy trying to get noticed?" He didn't wait for an answer, letting the door shut behind him.

Jamie kept her eyes on her plate.

"We've got a lot to do, Andy. You stick close to the house and keep an eye out for the trucks moving in and out. Mind *Nurse Jamie*."

She caught him with his hand poised on the doorknob. "Don't forget your physical therapy is at ten thirty."

"I don't have time for that this morning."

"You do if you want to make it through the rest of the

day and night. Or do I need to ask Dr. Cuesta to weigh in on this?"

His gaze narrowed on her. "Okay, Nurse Jamie, I'll be here."

"Don't be late."

He didn't reply as the door shut a bit loudly behind him. That made her smile. And if he was unhappy now, just wait until he kept his appointment. It was going to be a good day.

THOMAS FELT LIKE a lame duck, standing on the sidelines and watching the men unloading the trucks of livestock that pulled in one after another. The stock that had been on the road with his siblings arrived and lined up in their usual rows. Each hand was well-versed in what needed to be done. They could manage without him, but that didn't sit well with him, either. He was just plain out of sorts, and he had a good idea why. That made it all the worse.

Coming downstairs and seeing his brother sitting so docile at the table and actually conversing with Jamie was a bit uncharacteristic. Truitt usually kept a distance with strangers…not because he was stuck-up or rude. He always kept more to himself, due to the scar he carried from his hairline down in a half-arc to just above his ear. It was a silent yet visible reminder of a tragic day that he saw every time he looked in the mirror. The rest of them carried their reminders inside them and that was hard enough. Strangers tended to stare a bit too long. Some were rude enough to question it. So Truitt just stayed on the periphery or hid under the rodeo-clown makeup.

"There's old hop-a-long." The cheeky remark was made by the rider that halted her horse a foot away from him, her sunglasses reflecting his glum stance back at him. The grin was more a loving smirk as she adjusted her seat in the saddle. "How goes it, big brother?"

"It was going fine until you came along with that smart remark."

"Hmmm, guess Truitt was right. You *are* a bear this morning."

"And yet you didn't heed his warning and steer clear."

"Now why would I resist such a temptation? Although I suppose I should cut you some slack…seeing as how you got hurt moving my bulls. Although if you had done it the way I told you to do so, you wouldn't have…"

"Don't you have someplace else to be? Maybe go buy some frilly outfit to tempt Gray to pay attention to you?"

The smirk faded a bit as she zoned in on him. "Me and frilly don't go well and you should know that. The last frilly thing I wore was that hideous prom dress you brought back from Dallas for me. But why would I need to tempt Gray?"

"Just that he's been around more than usual. Guess it doesn't have anything to do with my temporary nurse jailer."

"And that might be the nurse jailer that is standing behind you right now?" His sister bent closer to where he stood. Her words were a loud whisper. "Open mouth, insert big boot. Later, brother." She raised back into the saddle and smiled at a silent Jamie. "It's nice to finally put a face with the voice on the phone. Thanks for being such a saint with putting up with my big brother. And I apologize on behalf of our whole family, too. He isn't exactly the most diplomatic one of us."

"Next time the bulls get out, good luck getting them back," Thomas bit out, his grip tightening on the crutch. He swung around and faced a non-smiling female. She had evidently heard his unflattering remark. Just something else he'd need to deal with.

"Thank you, Tori. It's nice to meet you in person, also. Andy sings your praises. And thanks for the loan of these boots." She glanced down at the pair that had become second nature to her now. The scrubs and sensible walking shoes now remained in her closet. "I'll have them cleaned up and back to you in—"

"Nonsense. Consider them yours. I have a few dozen others. We'll visit later at the party. Have fun, you two!" She wheeled the big gray horse around and left them alone.

"I thought we had an appointment. You coming?" He had taken the lead up the path toward the house.

"*You* have an appointment, yes." She moved ahead of him once they reached the sidewalk. His hand reached out and pulled her up, fingers around her wrist. She looked at him in surprise.

"Look, what I said back there. That was just brother and sister banter. Tori ticked me off and I shot back at her. It wasn't meant to be personal. I'm sorry if you took it that way."

She considered his words, and it was tough to read her thoughts. It was a good sign that she hadn't jerked her hand away. It felt nice and he wasn't in a hurry to let her go. The contact was both soothing and frustrating at the same time.

"Well, I suppose I can understand that even though I never had a sibling to joke around with. And I hope you know that it's nothing *personal* what happens next, either."

That's when Thomas followed the path her gaze took. A tall, muscular man in navy scrubs stood on the porch waiting for them, a smile on his face. Before he could voice his question, Jamie supplied the answer.

"This is Randall White. He's head of the physical therapy department at the hospital. He owed me a favor and agreed to come out today and give you a really good workout. I thought you'd like a change of pace. Isn't that nice of him?" The smile she gave Thomas was too sweet. She had turned the tables on him and was enjoying every moment of it. He freed her hand.

"I promised to take Andy into town with me on errands. I'll leave you both to it." She paused next to Randall and in an aside that could be heard by Thomas, she added, "And don't hold back. He's a real *tough* cowboy, this one."

By the time Jamie and Andy returned from town, the smell of mouthwatering barbecue on massive fire pits on trailers situated next to the open-sided show arena was mingling with other aromas of pork and caldrons of pinto beans. Long tables were being covered in red and white gingham tablecloths for the platters of side dishes and desserts held in the hands of couples and families arriving for the big event. Parking her car in one of the few open spaces close to the house, she and Andy made haste with their sacks through the back door and into the kitchen where Dottie and Tori and some of the wives of the ranch hands were busy.

"Thank heavens you're here," Dottie said, taking one of the bigger bags from Jamie's hands. "We can't have a party if the guest of honor isn't here."

"That's me!" Andy piped up as he passed his box of goodies off to Tori.

"That's right, and you better skedaddle upstairs young man and get into the shower and then into your party duds." Tori ruffled his hair as she swiped the hat off his head and put it on a peg beside the doorway. "Inspection will be in thirty minutes down here."

"I'm gone." And he was off like a shot up the back stairs.

"I'm sorry, Tori. We had to go to three different stores to find enough of the strawberries you wanted. Then Nelson's supply truck was just being unloaded, and it had the items on your veggie tray list. Everything seemed to be working against our timetable."

"Don't worry. You made it, and now you need to not worry about anything but getting yourself ready for the party, too. We've got this."

"Okay, I'll go change. But I'm an extra pair of hands tonight, not a guest."

"No argument… Move, young lady." This came from a Dottie who sent her best "drill sergeant" look across the kitchen at her. Jamie didn't say another word.

Seeing what most of the women were wearing, Jamie was glad she had taken a quick look through the boutique next to the produce store while they had to wait for the items they ordered to be ready. She was never one of those women who enjoyed long afternoons of shopping. She knew what she wanted on sight, and once done, she was glad to put it behind her. She knew she was going to wear the lemon-yellow off-the-shoulder blouse with the wide eyelet ruffle around the neckline. The debate was between the white just above knee-length skirt or the dressy white jeans. In the end, she chose the skirt with a slender gold chain belt around the waist. Gold hoops were the only nice jewelry she owned, and they went well with the belt. She had a pair of white and tan espadrilles that made her legs look not half bad, she had to admit, as she made another turn in front of the mirror.

A light touch to her makeup and then she decided she'd leave her hair loose but caught upward on the sides with two combs. She didn't know why she was taking so much care with her appearance. She planned to be more kitchen help than one of the guests. It couldn't be because she wanted to show a certain mule-headed rancher that she owned more than scrubs and could look human once in a while. *Nope.* That couldn't be it. Although she had tried to keep the memories of his kisses and her response far from her brain, it was more often than not a losing battle. Since he had neither mentioned it nor made any other advances, he had evidently decided he had made a mistake.

Besides, she'd be going back to her real life in a matter of days. And she knew the power of regrets and how they could mess with a person's mind. She had tried to not put herself into situations where there could be a chance of that happening. No entanglements, no regrets…no chance of a broken heart.

Chapter Nine

"I'VE GOT A couple of extra ropers I want to run through this afternoon," Thomas said, leaning against the entrant table and adding some notes on the run sheets. They had opened their arena up to area ranches to bring along any roping or barrel horses they wanted to test out or show off to any perspective buyers in the crowd of partygoers and fellow horsemen.

"What was all that racket I heard this morning coming from down the hall in the direction of your bedroom? At first I thought my brother was finally taking a page from my playbook, but then it sounded too painful toward the end…not pleasurable at all. Or maybe you're just out of practice."

Thomas looked up to see his bronc-busting brother, Trey, saunter up to join him and Truitt. "Nice of you to join us today. You just crawling out of bed?"

Trey shot a half-amused grin at Truitt's remarks. "I have you know I already was up, thanks to our brother's hollering. And Tori calling me every five seconds to remind me to pick up the package at the leather goods store this morning. A guy can't get any rest around here."

Truitt shot a look at Thomas. "Hollering? You weren't giving Nurse Jamie a hard time of it this morning were you? I'm surprised she's managed to not pour a bucket of water over your head or even dump a cup of coffee in your lap. You weren't very hospitable this morning."

"Another convert? Seems Nurse Jamie just keeps adding to her list of admirers."

"Nurse Jamie? She sounds like a pretty smart lady if she's got your number already. And I…" Trey's voice stopped abruptly and his whole body straightened to attention. Truitt and Thomas followed his gaze. A smile actually creased Truitt's mouth while the opposite was apparent from Thomas.

"Who in the world is that filly on our range and why haven't I met her already?"

Thomas snorted in disgust at his brother. "I'd like to see you try to smooth talk that 'filly.' She's one aggravating thorn under a saddle. Nurse Jamie isn't all sweetness as she appears."

Trey and Truitt both looked at their older brother, but neither said anything. The next look they shared with each other spoke volumes. Truitt stayed silent but not Trey.

"Well, well…maybe I'll just introduce myself and see what medical advice she might have for this banged-up cowboy. You sit back and watch a master at work, big brother." Trey was already sauntering toward the cake table where the nurse in question was placing streamers around its edges.

Trey stepped right up and off came his Stetson; that mega-watt smile was in full force. Nurse Jamie smiled right back.

"Yep...I'd say our little brother hasn't lost his charm with the ladies. But he best watch out. I think she's too smart for the likes of him. And I'd hate to see him land those new jeans of his in a pile of fresh cow manure when he wakes up in one of the pastures." Truitt didn't smile as he watched the pair.

Thomas slowly shook his head. "You spent what, fifteen minutes with her this morning in the kitchen, and you're a devotee, too?"

"I think I'm a good judge of character. And so is your son. Besides, she didn't even blink an eye when she looked at me or miss a beat of conversation. I guess being in her line of work, she's seen worse. I'm just saying either fish or cut bait, brother, as our dad would have said if he were here right now. Or you might be left holding an empty fishing rod." Truitt left him standing as he headed off toward the chutes and cattle pens. But he had to leave those pearls of wisdom in his wake. Thomas frowned. And then he squared his shoulders and headed in the direction of that cake table. He had his own choice words for his nurse.

"So you're the Florence Nightingale that's earned the badge of courage for putting up with my oldest brother. I have heard your praises sung by my nephew long before this moment. I'm Trey Tremayne…the handsomest Tremayne brother." His smile eased into a grin that could definitely knock a girl's better judgment into the ditch if she didn't know better. Jamie knew better. She accepted the hand he offered in a firm, yet non-predatory grip.

Jamie gave an answering smile. "The handsomest? Do each of you own a superlative?"

"Of course. The wisest would be Truitt—still waters run deep and all that stuff. And then there's Tori—the prettiest and most stubborn. She gets two since she's a girl."

"And your other brother?"

Trey shook his head. "He would be the oldest. And I'll leave it at that because he's listening." He gave a nod to the figure who stood a few feet behind her, arms folded across his chest and his gaze dead on the pair.

"Pops could use a hand with the ice chests…if you can tear yourself away."

"Well, since it's Pops and not mucking out stalls duty, I'm on my way. But I will be claiming some of your dances this evening," he said with a smile at her.

"And you might want to give her hand back now." The reminder was dry as a bone.

Trey just grinned more. He released the palm he held slowly. "I am very glad to meet you, Jamie. This is going to be enjoyable to watch." With that he touched the brim of his hat with a finger and sauntered off in the direction of the cooking pits.

Jamie waited for the hammer to be dropped. She knew it would come due to her little prank earlier that day; she just had no idea what form it might take. She met the cowboy's gaze head-on, her hands keeping a tight grip on the rolls of streamers now held in both hands.

"Sorry to tear him away from you."

"No problem. I've seen my share of flirtatious cowboys before." Jamie waited. She wished he would just get it over with.

"Well, my brother always did have an eye for searching out the prettiest girl in a crowd." Then he turned away and left her staring at his retreating backside, which was a very nice sight given the way his dress jeans fit his lower half. But she pushed that thought away as quickly as it had popped up. She was confused. He hadn't lowered the boom on her about his physical therapy session. He had simply given her a compliment and then left. A very nice compliment. Her gaze narrowed.

"What is he up to?" Her words were just above a whisper, but she received a response that made her jump. Tori had come up beside her, her gaze following Jamie's, and she shook her head.

"Funny…my other brothers and I've been asking ourselves that since we heard about you. After making some observations, I, for one, am very glad to see this interesting development with dear Thomas." Her words were cryptic and delivered with a saucy wink. She took the rolls of streamers from Jamie and began to place them where they were meant to be before Jamie got sidetracked.

Jamie had to set the record straight. She didn't want anyone getting the wrong idea. "I'm not sure what interesting development you're referring to, but he is healing and should be fine without a crutch by the end of the week. Then I can return to my usual duties at the hospital."

"That's good to hear." Tori handed her one of the rolls, and they began to work together. "So what do you think of the Tremayne men? And don't think you have to be socially correct or anything. I'm their sister and know all their worst secrets."

"Well, off the top of my head, I'd say that you're very lucky…in spite of knowing their secrets," she had to admit. "I haven't seen you all together that much, but from what little I have and what I've heard, you're very lucky to have such a close-knit family. I envy that. I hope you know how blessed you all are to have each other…even in the most aggravating of moments."

Tori paused and gave her comments some consideration. "You know…you're right. We could have lost so much more a while back. And I do thank God each day that I have my brothers and our home and the life we want. I just want my brothers to be happy. Thomas and Andy perhaps most of all." She returned to her decorating, but that didn't keep her silent.

"Thomas can act like a hard case. He has to. He's the boss man of this whole operation. He makes it possible for the rest of us to leave and not worry about the home fires. He keeps this ranch and all its parts running like a machine. And he manages to make time to be a great dad and sometimes a loving brother…when he isn't playing matchmaker or some such nonsense."

"Yes, he does have a tendency to do that. He's shared with me on more than one occasion there seems to be plans for a special match between you and a member of local law enforcement. Forgive me if I am overstepping there."

Tori shook her head and a sigh escaped her. "Thomas thinks Gray and I have an understanding or some such nonsense. We've been friends since grade school. He's practically an adopted brother."

"I see. I thought there was a romance there. And I didn't just get that idea from your brother. Gray seems to be a very nice person."

Tori's gaze swept over the growing crowd of people. Her eyes stopped on one area. It didn't take Jamie long to locate the point of interest. Gray Dalton, in uniform and Stetson, stood a few inches above most of those around him. He was busy returning greetings and comments with the guests. She saw the look in Tori's baby-blue eyes. *Yep, she's got it bad.* But for whatever reason, the timing was not right for her to admit it to herself. A slice of envy shot through Jamie. She reminded herself that she was the outsider looking in.

"I have the packages from the family sitting just inside the tack room door inside the arena. When we're ready to bring out the cake, I'll get a couple of the hands to carry them out. Andy's other gifts are on the kids' tables under the trees in the backyard. The pool opens in a few minutes, and the kids will be entertained for a couple of hours. I'm glad that we were able to find a couple of lifeguards to put there. Then the food comes off the pits and we can all eat. You'll have a group hanging around the arena to watch the action there. Then we'll bring out the steaks to go on the pits for the evening round, along with a good local country band for some boot-scootin'. You do like to dance, don't you? Because I know a few dozen ranch hands that plan on signing your dance card. And a brother or two."

Jamie noted the last part…perhaps two of Tori's three brothers might ask her to dance? The third one had to be Thomas. He'd steer clear of her. And that was fine. She had hoped to escape to her room with a good book. Parties were never her thing. Once Andy blew out his candles and opened his presents, she'd planned to slip away.

The *idea* of slipping away slipped away once the activities began. There turned out to be a handful of scrapes and bruises from kids getting into the action in the pool and play area. Then a couple of "chefs" got too close with their hot pits and needed attention. And one of the cowboys landed harder than planned from a new horse that got spooked by rambunctious steers in the holding pen. A dislocated shoulder was quickly reset, and the tough rancher was back on the horse in no time. Jamie shook her head and headed toward the drink table, only to be brought up short.

Thomas's familiar figure was headed her way down the stone path. She had managed to stay under the radar for a couple of hours. But it looked like her luck had just run out. He didn't break stride but came straight up to her, stopping a foot or so away. He held two glasses in his hands. One he held out to her.

"Sweet tea, extra on the ice. You've been a bit busy so I figured you could use it about now."

Jamie didn't know what surprised her more—the fact he had noted how busy she had been, or knew how she liked her tea? Either one was just as confusing. She took the tea with a grateful smile and nod. "Thanks, you read my mind."

"And you need some shade. I reserved you a quiet spot. Follow me."

He left her no choice but to follow in his wake. She was intrigued. He was up to something. Just what it might be, she had no idea. But she'd go along for a bit.

The path was one that led around the main ranch house and up a little rise to a grouping of trees that gave natural shade to the round rock patio area. She was surprised to see that an A-framed yard swing had appeared in the space that before that day had been just an empty spot. She felt the soft breeze moving over the slight rise, and the shade was quite nice. He held the swing in place while she took a seat. Then he sat down, the space between them smaller than what she would have liked for her peace of mind. She could feel the heat of him through the thin material of her skirt. A deep breath was in order along with a long sip of her tea.

They sat in companionable silence for a few moments, sips of tea their only movements. When one long arm moved to rest nonchalantly along the back of the swing, Jamie felt like a little fly caught on the edge of a spider's web, hopeless to flap around and try to get free now as the predator took its time stretching out the inevitable.

"Thank you for the tea. And the shady spot to relax. This is a perfect place for a yard swing. And I suppose you're trying to make me feel bad about the little switch in your physical therapy routine this morning."

"Well, now that *you* mention it that was a bit of a surprise. I suppose it was getting back at me for my behavior at the swimming hole. Which, by the way, I won't apologize for."

"The swimming hole…" she began and then stopped. He was referring to the kiss. She needed to set him straight on that point. "It had nothing to do with the swimming hole. It's always good to have another therapist's opinion and expertise on a case. He agrees that you're just about back to 100 percent. And maybe it was just my way of playing a tiny bit of a joke on you." She had to relent a bit.

"Good, because the crutch is definitely in the way. In fact, I have no idea where I left it, so it's just as well."

"I'm sure we can find it or another one for you."

"You never give up, do you? Being the perfect nurse and always so cool and calm and in charge. Do you ever have a bad day, Nurse Jamie?"

She didn't answer right away. She looked to the far-off mesas shimmering in the late afternoon heat waves. Her silence was not lost on the man beside her.

"I stuck my foot into something again."

"I have my bad days same as everyone else. And sometimes worse patients than others come along."

"And where would you rate me as a patient? Be honest if you dare."

"You're on a sliding scale. You began in the top spot. Then you began a slow…*very* slow…slide down the scale. Now, you're hovering around the mediocre four or five position."

His gaze was coolly assessing of her. She could feel it. But she preferred to keep hers on a distant point.

"I can't quite figure you out. It's like you're one of our skittish fillies, standing apart, then inching closer with the rest. Then something sends you scooting away, out of reach. Did someone hurt you in the past? Could that be it?"

She shot him a look and would have risen if his hand hadn't laid claim to hers as it lay on the swing between them. There was no teasing glint in the dark blue depths that searched hers.

"I'm not a horse. I'm just a private person. Not everyone can be the life of the party."

"Nice try. Trying to divert the conversation away again. But I find the mystery of you intrigues me."

That's why he had shown an interest. She wasn't the usual female who fell for the Tremayne charms. And she was nothing more than a diversion to amuse himself with as he dealt with being semi-incapacitated. Just a way to pass the time until she was gone; he wouldn't even remember her name in another month…if that long. She stood but his hand kept her tethered to him.

"Don't let me keep you from your host duties. I'm sure there are many people who want your attention." He stood next to her…much too close. The air became harder to take into her lungs.

"But you're not one to want it."

"Why are you doing this? This flirting, for want of a better word. And why me?"

"Why not you? I asked around and there doesn't seem to be a beau in the picture. Unless you have a husband hidden some place other than Faris, no one knows about him. Do you have any deep dark secrets, Nurse Jamie?"

She bit her tongue, because for a split second she wanted to blurt out *yes!* What would he think about her then? Just how suitable would she be for someone like a Tremayne? She came from a poor family. She had no idea who her real father had been. Jamie doubted her mother had even known for certain. But it was the stepfather who came into her life at the age of six that thrust them into a living hell. The fact that he had killed her mother, and she had been the sole witness at age ten... Now just how would that be for a conversation starter with the likes of a Tremayne?

Why did she ever have to kiss him? It opened a box of *what ifs* and *why nots* that never could be. And why was that blasted song "Over the Rainbow" playing softly from someone's radio or phone and drifting over to where they stood? How rotten was the timing? There was no perfect place over the rainbow or anywhere else...not in her experience.

"I can't seem to help myself." The words were whispered against her lips as he lowered his head. She stood still as a statue, for to do otherwise would have broken whatever spell had taken over the two of them. "From a scared doe to a look of such deep sorrow... Your eyes are speaking volumes right now and I can't help myself." Those words were muffled against parted lips as he lifted away for just a moment and then reclaimed her mouth with an added layer of need.

Jamie was helpless. *For just a few seconds more...*the words kept repeating. For a little longer she could pretend. All was perfect in the world, and Thomas would go on kissing her forever. Forever never did last long enough. It was the sound of kids' laughter that brought them both back to earth. Three guilty spies ran off when they saw they had been discovered from their vantage point in one of the fuller hedgerows. That left one smiling in place. And it had to be Andy. "This is the best birthday ever!" Then he was off like a rocket to find his friends no doubt.

"I was afraid of this," Thomas said, a frown knitting his brow as he looked after the departing figure of his son. "I better go find him and nip whatever fanciful ideas he has in his head in the bud before this goes too far. I'll catch up with you later. We definitely need to talk."

Jamie gave what she hoped was a positive smile and a nod. She watched Thomas walk away. *And perfect never lasts very long.* Absently, two fingers touched her lips where his warmth was fading. *A fanciful idea indeed. Before it goes too far…*his words reminding her to keep her feet planted firmly on the ground.

Chapter Ten

"I'VE BEEN SENT to find you and get you out there for Andy's cake cutting." Truitt came into the kitchen, and his stealth made Jamie jump at the sound of his voice.

She turned and smiled at the tall man. "I guess I just got so busy in here, I lost track."

"No offense, but I recognize a fellow recluse when I see one. I think that's about excuse number three on the list of why one doesn't want to be around people at the moment. But you *are* missed, and I did promise the birthday boy that I'd deliver you."

He had her there. She nodded. "You're a very smart man. I think your sister told me you were the wise one of the Tremaynes. She was right." Jamie hesitated and then spoke again. "May I ask a personal question…since it's just you and me in here being fellow recluses?"

He held still for a moment, his eyes on the brim of the hat held in his hand, fingers running absently along its edge. "I figure since I ferreted out your hiding spot, I owe you one."

"We all have our reasons for not wanting to be around

people, as you put it. Would yours have something to do with the scars you carry?"

"You did notice earlier…just too polite to ask the inevitable question or too polite to be repulsed enough to turn away."

"Politeness, maybe, because that's how I was raised. Repulsed? Sorry, I've seen a lot worse. In fact, I truly didn't notice right away. I think we often believe our imperfections are much worse than they might be…for a variety of reasons I'm sure you've heard if you've spent any time after your family's tragedy in counseling sessions. I won't pretend to be a psychologist. But I can speak the truth and no woman with any brains would ever find you repulsive. That is my two cents for whatever it might or might not be worth."

Truitt looked at her with something that was a mixture of respect and amazement and appreciation. "Well…it might have more worth than you guess. And the other truth is that you're too amazing to be stuck in a kitchen. Shall we?" He held out his arm for her to take. She slipped her hand around it with a sincere smile.

"Two kindred spirits. Lead the way."

It wasn't lost on Jamie as they approached the gathering and Truitt led them to the front and stood protectively beside her, that another pair of Tremayne eyes watched their every move with interest. Jamie did not dare look in Thomas's direction. She kept her attention on the little boy as the group sang the birthday song. There was applause and laughter as he managed to blow out all the candles on the top of the cake. Just before he did though, he paused and clamped his eyes shut with a fierce set to his jaw. Whatever he wished for was obviously very important. Then he opened and blew out every single candle. Tori and Dottie took care of the cutting and plating of the huge sheet cake in its western motif.

Next came the lineup of gifts. Pop's was first, followed by Dottie's and then he opened Jamie's. It was by accident on her second evening at the ranch she had come across Jasper listening intently while Andy read to him a story of cowboys and the Wild West. When she asked him about it, it was clear he loved reading and was quite good at it. That's when she decided his gift would be a set of books that featured a dog much like Jasper and his owner a young boy much like Andy. It was quite popular she was told by the librarian who helped her find the set for purchase online. Andy's face broke into a wide smile, and he ran around the table to grab her around the waist in a heartfelt hug. Her heart was overwhelmed in that moment, and she realized just how hard it was going to be to not have such a little man in her life much longer. She was grateful when he returned to the table and the next gift. Thomas's gaze had been thoughtful as he watched the two of them.

When the Tremaynes did something, they did it in a big way. The birthday party for a seven-year-old boy was major by anyone's standards…at least in the world Jamie came from. But the siblings had topped his day off to beat them all. His horse was led out, and Andy's eyes couldn't get any bigger in his face. The hand-tooled leather saddle had been especially made for him, with initials stitched into leather, along with the ranch brand. The bridle and reins matched it perfectly. That was from his dad. There was a smaller box from Trey that held a smaller replica of the silver World Champion belt buckles that the three men of the family all sported, along with a pair of silver spurs. The box from Truitt that went with it contained a pint-size pair of leather chaps with the brand of the ranch down one leg and the prerequisite fringe. There was a brand-new roper's rope he added. The last box came from Tori, and Jamie heard Dottie tell a friend beside her that it was a Tremayne tradition. At age seven they had each been given their first pair of special boots and it was Andy's turn.

The crowd was suitably impressed. Jamie was amazed at the workmanship. Andy was speechless as his hand rubbed over the pair of brown leather boots that had been especially made for him…his initials and the brand also featured among the swirls and artist cuts up and down the shafts. Then Tori and his dad earned hugs much the same as Andy had given her. As people pressed forward to get better views of the bounty, Jamie stepped back. For some reason there were tears in her eyes and that was silly. Her heart was full for the little boy, surrounded with so much love from his family and their hundreds of friends, most of them lifelong.

They were all part of the same fabric and would be through generations to come. She couldn't imagine what it must feel like to be so connected to the past and present and future.

"Why the tears?" Thomas had come after her as she tried to make her way back toward the house. "Do you not feel well? Is something wrong?"

Jamie blinked away the moisture and tried to make light of it all. "It was just a dose of the smoke from the pits and the wind kicking up a little dust. It's a great party and Andy is a blessed little boy. You all are very blessed. I need to see how I can help in the kitchen." She went to turn away, but a hand on her arm stopped her. Then the hand slipped downward and claimed hers.

"Nope. You are now off the clock and on guest time for the rest of the evening. And as this is my land, and my say-so...then that's that."

She could see that he was trying his best to bring some sort of smile to her face. In that moment, she knew she had just taken that final step off a very high cliff. How could she have prepared against it? The blue gaze was invading every ounce of space within and around the heart that was threatening to beat its way out of her chest. Thomas Tremayne...the second...held on to her hand as if it was his to have and to hold from that moment forward. What was scariest of all? She saw that he might be experiencing much the same thoughts. And they might just be as foreign to him as to her. The slight squeeze of his hand around hers came just as he whispered the words, "We've got this."

And she believed him. Caution went out the window as trust and a smattering of magical pixie dust came in. Maybe there might be a fairy tale waiting for her after all. *Close your eyes and make a wish.* And she did.

"SOMEONE DANCED THE night away and can still be up with the dawn? I am impressed." Tori's words met Jamie as she came into the kitchen and found the Tremayne sibling seated in one of the chairs at the round table in the corner alcove, a cup of coffee in front of her and the newspaper open wide.

"I'm usually an early riser. Force of habit, I guess." Jamie poured a cup and joined Tori.

"Of course, I never knew that my oldest brother had moves on the dance floor, either. Last night was a revelation to all of us. Guess he was just inspired…by something or someone." Her grin spoke volumes across the table. "Don't get me wrong. I think it is absolutely great to see that Thomas has finally taken some advice and jumped into the land of the living and all things possible such as romance and wedding bells and—"

"Leave the poor girl alone, Tori. Why is it that a man dances more than three or four times with the same female and immediately it means a preacher is to be called and a wedding band stuck through his nose?" Trey had joined them. He looked a little worse for the morning hour. He grabbed a couple of aspirin along with his coffee. Turning one of the chairs at the table around, he straddled it, downing the pills and a swig of the coffee as a chaser.

"My, my, aren't we all roses and sunshine this morning? You do realize that we've got stock to load out and get on the road, right? And then you hit the road for the next month and a half. I'd lay off the party circuit if I were you... There's two or three cowboys not far behind you in points. I'd hate to end up in Las Vegas with me in the arena and you sitting in the stands."

The look he shot his sister said words that Jamie was glad he didn't voice. Tori just smiled at him. "Love you, too."

"The sun's up and you can just sit and drink coffee? Those bulls of yours aren't loading themselves, Tori." That came from the man entering the room followed by a pint-size version of himself...dressed in brand-new boots and chaps. The belt buckle was even shinier than Jamie remembered from the party. Had he been polishing it already? It wouldn't surprise her. When she had followed Thomas upstairs as he carried a much too-tired-to-party-anymore little boy in his arms, they had worked to get his pajamas on him, but no way would he let go of the buckle. Jamie had tiptoed ahead of Thomas from the room.

"Something's put a smile on Nurse Jamie this morning. At least one pleasant face at the table to look at. Too bad

Andy and I had our breakfasts and been out to the pens once already." His smile held a special warmth that caused Jamie's cheeks to grow warm under the steady regard of the people in the room.

"And my guess might be that it's the same reason that put you in such a good mood this morning…if I was going to comment at all." Tori couldn't help teasing her oldest sibling.

"And you should be seen and not heard…or not seen at all even, because it's your precious Max being loaded next." He hadn't finished the sentence until she was out of the chair and grabbing for her hat. She tossed a look across at Jamie.

"I promised to introduce you to the special man in my life. Come along if you want to meet him."

Jamie nodded. She was glad to leave the men behind and Thomas's knowing glint as he followed her exit across the room. As they neared the stock pens, the area was a moving mass of men on horseback and on foot. Metal gates were clanging open and then shut amid shouts at animals. Stock trucks lumbered in empty and then were filled with mooing, stomping cargo. The high-pitched whinnies of the bucking stock were mixed in with the group, and Jamie stayed glued to Tori's side for fear of stepping outside an imaginary safe zone.

"You can perch on that top rail beside Pops. He's doing a count on the sheets in his hands. You'll be safe up there among all this craziness. My head would be on the chopping block if I let anything happen to you. That's the thought my brother telegraphed loud and clear to me as we left the kitchen."

Jamie took her designated spot and ended up helping Pops with the numbers and keeping eyes out according to his instructions. In between, she was able to ply him with some questions; he was very patient with her novice inquiries. She learned that there could be more than one stock contractor for a large rodeo. The best ones were kept busy and on the road for months out of the year. Tori was quickly earning a name on her own with her bucking bulls. In fact, her baby and pride and joy was in the running for one of the top spots at the National Finals in the next year or two if all stayed on track.

"So both the cowboy and bull or bronc earn points given by the judges? And the points add up to money and standings to see who get to go to these Finals?" Jamie reiterated beside him.

"That's the short of it. And only the best come out on top after all the months of racing from one rodeo to the next, often times with broken bones wrapped up tight and stitches here and there."

"Why do they want to do that? Do those buckles mean that much?"

"To a rodeo cowboy it does. The bragging rights mean more. Not everyone gets to wear one of those World Champion buckles. The cowboy or cowgirl who does earned it through lots of sweat and hard work, giving up family time and living on the road, often in the back of their pickups or stock trailers. Eating meals at truck stops or bologna sandwiches they slap together as they drive from one rodeo to another...sometimes making three or four rodeos in a weekend. It's all about adding up those points and getting enough to be in the National Finals in December in Vegas. The ones who wear the buckles earned them and then some. And the stock contractors...to have your animal chosen to go against the best of the best riders in the country... well that's an honor not very many get to experience."

"And yet you never wanted to be out there on the road with them? You stay here at the ranch and look after all the rest of it."

"I rodeoed in my teenage days. But I figured out early on that I didn't have that edge it takes to be on the level with the champs who made a living out of it. I was more of the cowpuncher than being the one the cow punched back at...if you know what I mean." He laughed at his own joke. Jamie grinned.

"Hey, Jamie," Tori called to her as she motioned a hand from the window of her pickup. "Want to ride over and see my babies?"

"Later, Pops," Jamie said, dropping down from the fence. "Thanks for educating me this morning."

"Anytime. I'll be around."

She slid into the passenger seat and Tori took off. "Has

Pops been bending your ear with his stories?"

"I think it was the other way around. He explained a lot to me about rodeos and events and points and all. I find it really interesting. I hope I didn't bother him too much."

"Pops loves talking anything cowboy. Bet he didn't share, though, that he and his family are in the Cowboy Hall of Fame? They are considered real pioneers in the ranching world. Not too many people have half the knowledge he does in that brain of his. We love him dearly."

"I think the feeling is mutual from what I've seen. He's proud of each and every one of you. And Andy gives him great joy. Does he not have a family of his own? He never married?"

Tori shook her head. "Pops gave his heart one time and one time only."

"What happened?" Jamie asked and then amended it. "I'm sorry; it's none of my business."

"If you're going to be around this family as much as I think you just might be, then it's natural to be curious. Pops showed up at the ranch looking for work after his family kicked him out when he was fifteen. Our aunt Sal, who is on the cruise and you haven't met yet, talked her husband into hiring him. He learned everything there was to know about every inch of this place. He was the best foreman out of any. He often said that he never found a woman who could both put up with him and his stubborn ways and life on a ranch in the middle of nowhere. He just became the confirmed bachelor. Although…there does seem to be one ranch woman who tends to give him some soft looks whenever she's around, but he pays no mind that I'm aware of." Tori turned off the road and they bumped over a cattle guard. "And you know the lady in question. It's just sad when two people were meant to be and yet, they just can't quite connect."

Jamie looked at the girl beside her. Was she talking about Pops or about someone else? Perhaps her situation with Gray? Or was she alluding to Thomas and her?

"Wait, you said I know this person who is sweet on Pops?" And the lightbulb suddenly came on in her brain. "You're talking about Dottie? Your neighbor?"

"Bingo. I think she's been sweet on him for a long time, that dates back even to when they were both young. But I just can't get a read on him to even guess if he knows or not." The truck pulled to a stop. A very fancy stock rig sat next to a loading pen. They got out of the vehicle and headed for the pen.

"Oh my heavens," Jamie whispered. "He's even bigger up close. I saw him from a distance after I first arrived here. He's enormous. And he's your *baby?*"

"I hand raised him when his mom broke a leg in a prairie dog hole and an infection set in and finally hit her kidneys. He was a little scrawny guy back then. I figured he needed a name to grow into. I chose Maximus. And he is a true gladiator at heart." Then she dropped her voice and whispered the rest. "But he's a soft marshmallow when no one is looking… Only that's our secret, so don't tell." She grinned and dug into her back pocket. She opened her palm flat and stuck it between the slats of the metal fencing.

"Here you go, sweet one. Your treat for the road. Come meet a new friend. This is Jamie and we like her. Come on," she coaxed in a soft voice. Jamie stood as still as possible in the spot next to her. As the huge bull eyed her, she began to rethink her idea of meeting an animal that could strike fear in a person by just looking at them, raising an eyebrow as if to dismiss them, and then trying to stomp their brains out. *Sweet one?* She wasn't so sure about that.

"Seriously, Tori," she said, still not taking her eyes off the animal. "Just how big is your little *sweet one?*"

"He's tipping the scales at just a few pounds over a ton."

Jamie's brain took it all in. "Well, perhaps if you didn't give him lemon drop candy as a treat, he might trim down a bit."

Tori laughed. "Well, the object is to add a few more pounds of muscle."

Then the animal began to move…and Jamie did her best to stand her ground. "Good gosh," she breathed as he came to stand a couple of feet away. His long tongue began to flick out toward the candy. "He's even taller than we are. He's massive. What idiot would want to get on his back?"

"One who wants to be the cowboy to say he rode a bull that had never been ridden before. Cowboys stand and salivate at that thought when he comes off the trailer."

Jamie looked at Tori's glowing face. "You really do love this animal. I can see it and hear the pride in your voice. I hope he gets you that buckle or trophy or whatever there is for having the best bucking bull. He certainly has my vote, and all he's doing is standing and eating candy."

"Thanks. He's special to me. For whatever silly reasoning in my brain, I guess I see us as kindred spirits. He lost his mom too early, and so did I. Maybe we have something to prove. And you probably think I'm even crazier now." Tori played her admission off with a laugh, wiping the last of the candies' stickiness on her jeans.

Jamie smiled and shook her head. "I get it. I don't think it's silly. Those of us who lost someone we love much too soon…well, it's not silly." She had caught herself and thoughts before finishing her sentence abruptly, hoping Tori didn't take notice. "But Maximus does have good choice in candy. I like that kind, too."

Tori grinned. "Well, it's a good thing I have another bag in the truck. Let's go get you some. And then it's time to get this big guy loaded and we hit the road again."

"On the one hand, it seems like it would be fun to be able to see the different parts of the country. But I guess on the other, being away from home and those you care about is hard, also."

Tori handed over the bag of candy from the glove compartment of the truck. Then she started the engine and put the truck into gear. They headed back toward the loading area. "It has its moments. And rodeo people and many fans are great people to get to know. But you can get homesick. I suppose it's a trade-off like any other job."

"Do you think you'll ever get tired of the road and want to stay closer to your home? Maybe want to have your own family and such?"

Tori gave it some consideration before responding. "A long time ago, I decided on my goal. And my dad told me that it meant long days and longer nights and a lot of proving myself to people in the business. Because unfortunately, there aren't that many of us females that want to do this sort of thing…raising bulls and being in stock contracting. But I'm not a quitter. I'm also hardheaded…just ask my brothers. But once I achieve my goals? Who knows? I'd like to have kids and a husband…when it's time. How about you? Ready for a husband and a child?"

And that was how easily the microscope was turned to Jamie's life. And she had a sneaking suspicion that Tori knew just what she was doing and was quite good at it. "I love nursing. It can have long hours and can take a toll on a person when you lose a patient or aren't able to separate the job and your private time. But, yes, like you said…when the time is right and the right person comes along. Who knows?"

Tori grinned over at her. "Yes, indeed. Who knows?"

Chapter Eleven

"Isn't it great? We're going to take you out on the ranch. And Dad and me picked out a really good horse for you to ride. Her name's Mischief Maker. She's the mom to my horse." Andy imparted the words as he skipped ahead of her toward the open doors of the first barn. Jamie wished she could mirror his enthusiasm. She had little recourse when faced with the news that the three of them were going on a little trail ride that afternoon after the siblings and trucks had pulled back out on the road.

Thomas had delivered the news with a smile that flipped something in the center of her chest and reminded her that she was in unchartered waters. At least Andy would be there to be an added buffer between the two of them…if she managed to even get on the animal, much less stay on its back.

"Smile, you aren't going to the dentist." She heard his words as she walked up to where he was cinching the saddle on one of three horses standing patiently tethered to their stall doors.

"That's easy for you to say. And right now, I'd argue a

visit to the dentist might be preferable."

"Are you afraid of horses or just afraid of having no experience with them?"

"I love horses. I just haven't had much experience with them in my life to date. Some of us weren't lucky enough to be born on a ranch." She met the blue-eyed gaze with a small lift of her chin. This was not her usual environment. She was an interloper.

"Well," Thomas smoothed into a grin, "I suppose I wouldn't be at ease in your hospital world." He turned to Andy. "Son, lead Red Bug on outside to the step gate and wait for us."

The little boy didn't need to be told twice. He looked so tiny next to the horse, yet the animal went in docile movements beside him, with Jasper on the other side.

"We should begin with introductions. Come closer. Horses pick up on your feelings, and she knows you're a novice. But you both have to be able to trust each other."

Jamie moved slowly toward the gray horse with the darker mane and tale. The animal watched her approach with an unblinking gaze from her almond-shaped black eyes. She reached out a hand, and with tentative strokes lightly moved up and down the nose that was presented to her.

"She's beautiful. Her eyes are gorgeous and such long lashes." Jamie laid her other hand on the horse's neck, smoothing along the short hairs. "You are such a sweetheart," she murmured to the animal.

She glanced over at the cowboy standing with his hand resting on the horse's back, his gaze still on her. "But why is she called Mischief Maker? That doesn't quite fit with the horse standing here right now. Is she just lulling me into a false sense of trust?"

He shook his head. "In her younger days, she had the habit of letting herself out of her stall and then doing the same to the other horses in the barn. Or she'd find her way into the tack room and rearrange the bridles and blankets or help herself to some oat snacks. Don't worry…her mischief was aggravating and the cause of joking. She didn't do any harm. Her gait is smooth and even as a rocking chair."

Jamie smiled at the animal. "I like your spirit there, girl. Keep people on their toes."

"Well, let's see how you feel about her once you get on her back. Put your foot here." He nodded to the stirrup he held in his other hand. "Remember, breathe. She can sense it if you're tense and afraid. Trust her to be your partner in this. Trust is the basis for every great relationship between horse and rider."

Jamie gave a skeptical look at the stirrup but moved slowly forward.

"Put your left hand on the saddle horn. Foot into the stirrup. The right hand goes to the back of the saddle seat. Take a push upward from your free foot and pull yourself up, your right leg swinging across her back and your foot into the other stirrup. On the count of three…"

Jamie held her breath, but concentrated on getting all the moving parts correct. To her amazement, the horse stood still. She made it into the saddle and then realized just how far down the ground was. But she had made it to that point. A smile of accomplishment curved her mouth.

"That was very good for your first mount." Thomas grinned, handing her the leather reins to hold. "You just might be a natural. Are you sure you haven't done this before?"

"I was six the last time I sat on a pony at the local carnival. It was tethered to a mechanical wheel that led her around in a circle, and I thought I was quite a cowgirl." She laughed at the memory.

"I bet. How many times did you ride that wild animal?"

That's when her grin stiffened into a smile. The memory had turned on a dime from a childhood keepsake to the remembered nightmare. Her mother had let her have three turns on the pony due to her begging. But then her stepfather had found them. He had put a quick end to it all, snatching her off the pony's back, berating her mother for spending his hard-earned money, and generally causing a scene before making them go to the truck and leaving the bright lights behind. She never asked to ride the pony again or any carnival ride for that matter. Lesson learned and never to be repeated.

"So how do I make this horse go?" She sat straight in the saddle and looked down at her teacher. He was watching her thoughtfully…and with a questioning light in his eyes, but he left the subject.

"Reins in hand, rest your hands just so." And his hand covered hers, his touch warm and almost gentle. It touched something inside her, and warmth settled through her. She didn't jerk her hand away as she might have in the beginning. "As you move, you'll keep your weight centered in the saddle and on the balls of your feet in the stirrups. Relax your knees against her side. She's going to learn your movements as you ride her. You'll learn that you can give her cues with your heels, pressure from your knees, directions in the reins."

"I knew it looked too easy from the spectator's seat," she said, pushing her nervousness back down inside.

Thomas took two steps and was in his saddle in one fluid movement. *Show off.* She envied him that ability. How long before she could do something like that? But why worry about that? She was leaving in two days. And Mischief Maker would be a sweet memory as she plied the halls of the hospital.

"Relax, Jamie. Mischief will follow along with the other two. I wouldn't have chosen a bronc for you…at least not for the first time." He grinned as her eyes flashed to his. "Let's go enjoy the day." He made a soft cluck and his big red horse moved off. Andy climbed on his pony, with the new saddle and bridle, from the top of what looked like a small step stool attached to the side of the corral fence. She would have appreciated that for herself.

Thomas led the way and Jamie had Andy next to her, keeping up a steady conversation. Jasper ran ahead now and then, but always came back to follow along a few feet from Andy. After they left the main ranch house area behind, they began to climb a bit along the base of the mesa that stood at the back of the main ranch buildings. Then they crossed a small trickle of a stream that she never guessed would have been there. Mischief did it with an easy stride, and Jamie gave her a thank-you pat on her shoulder. She was grateful she hadn't been unseated yet.

Trees were taller in the area they moved next, and she could catch glimpses of wide swaths of open pastures with green grass coverings and herds of black cattle dotting them. Jamie realized they were more or less following not too far from a dirt track of a road that crisscrossed the area. She didn't understand why they just didn't follow along in those tracks.

But Thomas was still riding silent ahead of them, and she decided that was a good thing. The less she had to talk to him, the less she had to watch his smile and feel that churning feeling in the pit of her stomach. It was difficult enough keeping her gaze on far-off points and her attention on what subject Andy was on at any given moment. She didn't need the added distraction of noting how good the rancher sat his horse, nor the way the hard muscles of his broad shoulders corresponded to the movements of the strong thighs hugging his horse's sides. *Yep.* It was definitely difficult not to admire his "seat" on the back of the animal.

"Mischief likes you. I can tell. If you watch her ears, you can tell what she's thinking," Andy was imparting next to her.

"That's good to know. I like her, too. You're very lucky to have these horses and to ride over such beautiful country. Are you going to be a rancher like your dad?"

The child grew quiet and looked to see how far away his dad was at the time. He just shrugged his shoulders. Jamie found that a change in the talkative little boy. "Is there something else you'd really like to do better?"

"Well…I really might like to do what my uncle Trey does. I want to ride broncs."

"Wow. That's a little different from working with cattle." Jamie realized the need to tread through an unseen mine field. "Why do you like that better than being a rancher?"

"It's fun. And you get to go to a lot of places. I know my dad could teach me to be a really good roper and all like he was…is, I mean. But I want to compete and win some buckles."

"I see. Well, you have a bit of time to truly decide on things. You might find you change your mind again."

"I guess so. That's what my uncle Truitt says."

"And what does your dad say about this plan?"

He shook his head. "I didn't tell him. I don't want to hurt his feelings. It's just something I'm thinking about right now."

She smiled. "I understand. And my lips are sealed. This is your business to discuss with your dad and no one else's."

"You're so cool, Nurse Jamie. I knew you were when you let me go into the hospital room and see my dad and didn't make a big deal out of it. You cook good, too. And you can take care of people like on a ranch in case they get hurt and all. You're real pretty, too. Even my uncle Trey said you were."

Jamie had to make an effort to hide her grin. "It sounds like you've made quite a list there. Thank you…I think."

"Seems he has." Neither of them had noticed Thomas had pulled his horse up and slowed to allow them to catch up. He sat watching them. "You and Jasper ride over to Rabbit Creek and see how the water is running. Then come back here, and we'll have the snacks that I brought along."

Andy's grin said it all. "Yes, sir. We'll check it out real good. And maybe I can catch one of the frogs to show Nurse Jamie." He set his mount off in a trot with Jasper racing ahead.

"Rabbit Creek is just across that pasture. He'll be in our line of sight the whole time. And I'll tell him to put the frog back if he finds one. I'm sure you aren't a frog type of girl." He stepped off his horse and allowed the reins to drop.

"Well, you don't know that I'm not that type of girl. I used to catch horned toads and carry them in my pockets."

Thomas stepped over to her horse's side and smiled up at her, a twinkle in those blue eyes. She forgot to look away. Her pulse did a bit of line dancing through her veins. "Now that is truly amazing. I wouldn't have ever guessed. I do enjoy uncovering those hidden secrets of yours. It keeps a guy on his toes. What else do you have to share?"

"My legs have gone numb and I may fall flat on my face if I don't get off this horse soon. Is it okay that I get off her now? I'm sure she'd appreciate it, too." She nodded at her horse who was standing so patiently.

"Put your hands on the saddle horn, slide your right foot out and over the back of the horse, and then take your other foot out of the stirrup."

Jamie did as she was told but her foot wouldn't come out of the stirrup, and she had to hop a couple of times to try to pull it free.

"Allow me," he said. "Just hold still and there you go." He held her steady and the foot came free. Then she went to take a step away and found a pair of rubbery legs almost sent her crashing to a heap at his feet, but he was quick and caught her.

"You weren't joking. Best let the blood get to circulating for a minute or two. When you get used to riding more, you won't have any problems."

And that's how she ended up in the one place that she

promised she wouldn't ever again…inside his arms. Her arms were caught between them, palms trying not to notice how solid he felt beneath them. She didn't think she would get control of her legs anytime soon if she remained where she was. They were feeling even weaker the longer she was held against him.

"Is it me that's making you so skittish or Mischief?"

She had no choice but to look up at him. She had never been one of those females versed in flirting with a male. What you saw was what you got with her. It had taken her quite a while to learn to look at any situation and not shy away from it. So she couldn't be coy now. He'd know.

"It's probably a 60/40 split."

Thomas threw his head back and laughed. Shaking his head, he returned his gaze to hers and this time, it was *all him* having the effect on her nerves and shortening her breaths. "And dare I ask which I am?"

"I think not. We'd hate for your head to get too big for your hat."

"I see my son heading back across the field. We'll have to postpone the rest of this interesting conversation. And by the way, I thought it might be time for you to get out more around here. I thought we'd drive over to McKenna Springs this evening. There's a very nice place to eat and do some dancing. I know you enjoy that after seeing you on the dance floor at Andy's party. Sound like a plan?"

He wanted to take her out. *Oh heavens.* She should say

no. But then, when would she ever get such an invite again? And they did have to eat…

"Good! No excuses. Thanks for the conversation." When she thought he was about to step away at the approaching sound of hoof beats, he paused and dropped a swift kiss on her slightly parted lips. When he raised his head, he gave a slow wink. "And let your hair down later." Then he stepped away and she was left to hope the pink in her cheeks wouldn't draw Andy's attention.

Thankfully, his attention was on the tiny green frog he cradled in his palm. While his dad took out the snacks he had brought along in his saddlebags for them, Andy sat beside Jamie on a fallen log and showed her the treasure. She had to admit that it was a cute little creature.

"Wow, Dad…she's even holding it. I bet other girls wouldn't do that."

"Well, not too many other girls are like Nurse Jamie. Or so I've heard a few times over the last three weeks or more." It was a tongue-in-cheek response, but Jamie caught sight of the smile. She also noted the slight limp he was trying to ignore as he had spread the blanket and placed the items on it. That would be her out…the excuse she would use to bow out of his plans for the evening.

But when that time came to use that card when they returned to the stables, she could just smile and nod when he mentioned the time they would leave. *Playing with fire.*

Chapter Twelve

"IN CASE I didn't say it earlier this evening, you certainly left Nurse Jamie at home tonight. And don't get me wrong, as much as I admire her...a lot...I have to say that the Miss Jamie Westmoreland standing here with me now, is a knockout."

When he had decided on his dinner plans earlier that morning, he hadn't thought it all out. But they had to eat, right? And he knew that Jamie wasn't exactly a party animal type of person. He had learned as much from observation and the fact that she admitted she had never been inside The Yellow Rose Dance Hall in nearby McKenna Springs. That was pretty much unheard of by the inhabitants of that part of the state. What cowboy in his right mind wouldn't take that advantage to show off the dance hall with one of the prettiest girls in the county on his arm?

In his right mind. That was the rub. He had asked himself what made him change his rule of staying away from her? Weren't things going just fine? *Not really.* That was the reply that kept coming right back at him as his heart and his common sense played ping-pong with each other. As much as he tried to hang on to that mantra and keep things on an even keel until she was gone, the more he felt himself losing a battle. In fact, he was fast losing the whole war.

But as he listened to his son's chattering away with their visitor on the ride earlier that afternoon—especially when he thought he couldn't hear them—something had hit him that was unavoidable. His son had made his choice known. Thomas should have known the day would come. But he hadn't counted on it being so soon. *Soon?* Was he serious? It had been just under seven years since his wife and Andy's mother had walked out on them. How hard would it be to raise his son and the two of them be all the other one needed? They were doing fine. Or so he thought. Then one day, Nurse Jamie, with the chocolate doe eyes and the smile of an angel that promised comfort and, he now knew, could also deliver sinful thoughts with the touch of her lips, had walked into their world.

As much as he fought it at first, he had to admit that the day she walked in their front door, it became tougher to think about her ever leaving. He had spent a few sleepless nights staring at the ceiling over his bed, looking for answers but not finding any. He was ignoring the one thing that was becoming much too clear. Maybe he had been wrong to keep a woman out of their lives. Maybe there was a good one, and she had come into their lives when least expected. He knew what Andy wanted and needed. But what did he want? What did he need? And there was just one answer that always came in the dead of the night...*Jamie*.

But he needed some answers and he needed to know her thoughts on the matter. Maybe she wasn't even interested. Maybe he was too long without a woman and couldn't get a good "read" on her responses to him. He was a man who didn't like to leave things on the table that needed to be finished. That included the conversation they needed to have at some point in the evening ahead.

Opening her door, he took her hand as she stepped down from the truck. The length of leg that came to light as the denim skirt caught on the edge of the seat dialed up his pulse rate. He approved of the off-the-shoulder frilly white blouse. It made him want to taste the sweet spots along her neck. He needed to keep his thoughts in control, or it could get embarrassing as his jeans grew tighter in his appreciation of the view before him.

He didn't relinquish her hand as they walked beneath the rose-covered trellis and skirted the pathway between the old Victorian inn and the flower garden that was a riot of color. The sound of other vehicles pulling into the expansive parking lot behind them mixed with the sounds of the country band playing a Shania Twain song. The smell of good food wafted on the cooling air of the approaching dusk. He felt a lightness both in his step and within him that he hadn't felt in a very long time. And it had to do with the woman walking beside him.

"I thought we might work up our appetites on the dance

floor a bit. Then find a quiet spot on the back patio over the river for some mouthwatering dish because I can attest to the fact that anything they cook here is downhome good."

She returned his smile along with a nod. "I think that's a good plan. You might as well find out right away about my two left feet."

"I'll be the judge of that. And besides, I think we managed okay the other evening at the party. I may still be a little rusty, too. I might just impress you by not stepping on your toes. You found out that my two brothers are a lot better on the dance floor than I will ever be."

The dance hall was the oldest in the state as the plaque beside its doors attested. The crowd inside and out on the patios was a mixture of young and old…ranchers, local businesspeople, college students from nearby Austin, families with children, tourists taking photos and learning to line dance. Open-screened windows ran the long length on both sides, and large fans suspended from the ceiling kept the air moving.

"There's no time like the present to jump in, pretty lady." With those words he twirled her once and then brought her into his arms. He led and she followed.

"And you said you couldn't dance?"

Jamie grinned. "I had no idea. But it seems the Tremayne men do know a bit about making their partners look good. I always tried to just be an observer from a safe distance when a dance floor is involved."

"Well, I think you won't get away with being a wallflower any longer."

"And I thought you said you weren't that good?" she responded.

"I guess we've both learned that you just need to find the right partner. You have to hold on tight and not let go." Neither one of them spoke after that, nor broke the gazes that tethered them together. The fast two-step changed into a slow waltz, and then a rousing "Cotton-Eyed Joe" woke up the group.

"One more and then we'll find something cold to drink and a menu?" He glanced down at the woman in his arms, and the change in her was mesmerizing. Her eyes glowed with enjoyment. Her cheeks wore soft color and her lips were parted in a heart-stopping smile. That's when he made his first misstep but quickly righted himself. She didn't seem to notice. *I won't let you go.*

"I think I agree with you."

"Excuse me?" He was trying to get his brain back into the moment.

"What you just said…about something cold to drink and food. I agree."

So he hadn't spoken his thoughts aloud…that made him release the breath he had held. He turned and led them off the floor and through the patio to the outside deck where they found a spot with a good view of the river flowing nicely below their cliffside table. Thomas was grateful for the menu the waitress handed him. He could use it to restore his equilibrium. *So this is how it feels?* Thomas had never been one to believe in the poetic musings of his siblings and the mush from the movies that basically touted bugles blaring and the world tilting on end to announce the arrival of cupid and his arrow.

Cupid and his arrow? He felt as if he had been hit between the eyes with a two-by-four and then drug around an arena by a runaway horse. He'd keep that description to himself. People might think he was truly off the rails. But he couldn't avoid the fact any longer. That illusive feeling called *love* had smacked him hard. He thought he was immune. So what was he going to do next? Where was the roadmap when he needed one? What if she couldn't feel the same way? His appetite had fled but he had to pretend that nothing out of the ordinary had happened…not yet.

MAYBE THOMAS WAS having second thoughts about their evening out? Perhaps she had been a bad dance partner and he was too kind to say so. He just seemed to have something on his mind as they began their meal. He smiled and spoke and did all the right things, but there was something she couldn't put her finger on. For a little while, on the dance floor, she almost believed that all sorts of wonderful things could happen after all. Jamie had spent so many years pushing such thoughts and hopes and dreams away, training herself to not count on anything but bad news. She stayed on alert, knowing that there were people in the world who could inflict the worst of pains on others and get away with it.

But this evening, she had told herself that she was going to enjoy just one evening without the past pushing in and without the future putting big question marks in her brain. Maybe Faris wasn't going to be her last stop along the road to find where she might belong, but right now, it was where she wanted to be…and Thomas Tremayne was part of that.

They decided to share one of the delicious slices of apple pie after their dinner plates had been cleared. She made it through four bites and had to give up. "Sorry, but the rest is up to you to finish. I am beyond full."

"I can agree, but my momma always made me clear my plate," he said with a grin. And the last crumb disappeared soon thereafter. "I think the dance floor is a bit crowded right now. Maybe we should walk this meal off. You like flowers? Let's check out the gardens. One of the owners has a fantastic green thumb."

A few minutes later, Jamie had to agree that his idea was a good one. "I envy the green thumb that created this kind of beauty. The roses are incredible. And their scent fills the air. Good choice."

"Thank you. I do have some good ideas now and then. And it helps that I heard you and Dottie talking about flowers one day as you two prepared dinner. I guess I filed it away for future reference. My mother always taught me to notice the little things. She said they are often the most important things."

"Your mother raised you right. And your brothers and sister seemed to have all turned out pretty great, too. She sounds like she was a very wise lady."

His blue eyes darkened but in a soft way. He nodded. "She was all of that and more. I wish I had told her that more often. Anything any of us have done good in our lives, is to her credit and my dad's, too. You have a spirit about you that reminds me of her at times."

"Spirit? I do?"

"She wasn't afraid to speak her mind and stand her ground when she felt she was right. And yet, she had this incredible comforting ability. She could sense when a person needed attention, maybe just a smile and some words to lift them up, or they might be in need of a helping hand. My father often said she was the compass of the family. She kept us all headed in the right direction. We just needed her to be around a bit longer. But then, we might be greedy, also."

She could see and hear the love and respect he had for his mother in his voice and in his eyes. It touched something in her heart that she had tried to bury with her past. It was a sad mixture of envy and loss, commiseration, and admiration. "I don't think it's greedy of you all to want more of what you lost. You can be thankful you had such parents. You were blessed."

"Well, I wish Andy could have had her longer in his life. He was six months old when we lost our family members. I try to tell myself that I should be thankful that she at least got to see my son for even a short time."

"You can be very proud of Andy. You've done an outstanding job raising him."

"Thank you. It wasn't always easy. My hat's off to single parents wherever they might be. I don't know what I would have done if my brothers and Tori, and Pops, Aunt Sallie, and other friends and neighbors hadn't been there for support."

"I can only imagine. I don't know the particulars, but I can't understand how any mother can walk away from her child. I know that I couldn't do that. But then, I haven't been in that person's shoes, either. I just know that Andy is quite an awesome little boy, and I enjoy being around him. I'll miss him when this assignment is done."

"I don't think I have to tell you that he's developed quite an attachment to you. It seems from almost the first moment he saw you that day at the hospital, he made a decision that you needed to be part of our lives. Don't tell me you haven't noticed?"

They were at the center of the garden, next to a small pond with a stone waterfall. There was a stone bench there and they seemed of the same accord to sit for a moment.

"He's a little transparent," she said, a smile appearing at the memory of the many times the child would make a remark...usually highlighting what a great guy his dad was and how much everyone was glad she was there. "I've tried to temper things a bit with him. But he can be very determined...something inherited from his father, perhaps." That brought a return smile from the man beside her. When his hand found hers on the seat between them, it felt natural for her to not pull away. *Small steps were sometimes the biggest.* A long time ago, her mother had told her that. Back when the future still shone in her mother's eyes.

"I'm aware you're probably being more than a little charitable. I know I acted like a jackass when we first met in the hospital, and that didn't improve much when I got back to the ranch those first couple of days. I'm sorry for that. I can only say that my opinion of having a female in our lives was the furthest thing from my mind when you happened along. Maybe I was being overly protective given the past." It was a sincere apology. And she knew it took a lot for him to admit it.

"You mean the past where your wife left. I can understand how difficult it can be to trust again once you've been through hell. And doubly so when you have a child involved. Apology accepted."

"That means a lot. And I can say that I realize you're nothing like Casey was. As different as night and day. I know I can trust you with my son's feelings."

His words both made her feel special and yet, there seemed to be something that still held her back. But she tamped it down and chose to take a chance. Maybe it was time to take more chances?

"And what about yours?"

"You do get to the heart of the matter. I knew you were something special the first time I looked into those doe-like eyes of yours. I just didn't know how special. Seems I find that I trust my son's judgment in this. And I trust in *you*." His kiss this time was sure and added as an exclamation point to his declaration.

His palm cupped her cheek as the kiss deepened, and Jamie felt her heart take flight in that magical garden as the moon rose above the trees and bathed them in silver. It was a night made for romance and dreaming and all things that suddenly made everything seem possible.

Chapter Thirteen

J AMIE OPENED HER eyes as the sun was peeking through the blinds in her bedroom. For the first time, she felt a smile on her face to begin the day. The image of a certain cowboy had a lot to do with that turn of events. Remembering the night before brought the warmth of a blush to her cheeks. Closing her eyes, she allowed her mind to relive certain moments. The gazes from those deep blue eyes had made her feel beautiful and special and cared for and about. Thomas made her laugh and feel as if she floated around the dance floor in his arms. And the kiss they shared in the moonlit garden… That was the first of a few more as he had driven them back to the ranch.

Just before they entered the house, he had pulled her into his arms one more time, and his palms molded her body to every plane and curve of his with hands that touched off wildfires wherever they caressed. Her own hands hadn't been bashful. Jamie couldn't remember ever feeling so alive, so desirable, and so needy all at the same time. Thomas had unburied a part of her she never expected to have anyone unlock.

He made it very plain with his hushed whispers against her cheek, his teeth lightly nipping at the sensitive pulse at the bottom of her neck what he would love to do if Dottie wasn't inside, waiting for their arrival. She had volunteered to be the designated babysitter, and perhaps it had been good that she had been there. It kept things in check. Because Jamie knew she would have been powerless if Thomas had taken her upstairs.

As it was, she sat up in bed, swung her feet to the floor, and stretched to greet the day ahead. There were two Tremayne men downstairs who would be gathering at the breakfast table. Her gaze swept over the clock on the bedside, and then she stood up in a hurry. She had overslept! Not a day to oversleep when she felt today was the beginning of something new and exciting…something she couldn't put her finger on. A change was in the air.

Jamie quickly showered, began to draw her hair back in a ponytail, and then stopped. She brushed it out and allowed it to flow freely across her shoulders and down her back. She dressed in jeans and a cotton shirt open over a blue tank top. She quickly put on a light lip gloss as she hurried down the stairs.

She caught the smell of coffee and bacon and the clatter of dishes as she passed through the dining room and stepped into the kitchen, where the broad smile altered somewhat when she realized that a guest had joined Thomas and Andy at the table. Pops was pouring her a mug of coffee, and she detoured to take it from him, a murmur of thanks meeting his "morning." Gray Dalton nodded at her.

"Good morning, Miss Jamie. Hope you don't mind me dropping by so early today. I had some business to talk over with Thomas."

"Of course not. Why should I mind? It's good to see you, Sheriff."

Her gaze finally made it over to Thomas. He returned it, but the warmth of last night didn't seem to be in full force. She knew he wasn't a man to wear his feelings on his sleeve, so she chalked it up to the guest in their midst. Jamie wasn't ready to allow the little voice of doom and gloom to take foothold in her brain.

"I have a plate with biscuits and bacon in the warmer waiting for you. Sit down and take some time to eat your breakfast. Andy just finished up, and he's going to be helping me out in the barn this morning with some chores. Then we need to run to the feed store in town. You just have to keep an eye on this patient here who might have overdone it last night on a dance floor or so I'm told." He produced the plate and motioned to the empty chair at the table. She didn't want to appear rude, so she slid into the seat next to Andy and across from Thomas.

"We're going to get some special shining stuff for my new saddle. Then I can keep it really nice every day. Just like the other hands do their stuff. A cowboy has to take good care of his stuff, so it lasts a long time."

It was clear that Andy was repeating information that he had taken to heart. He was proud to take another step closer to being like the "big ranch hands" who he wanted so badly to emulate. Jamie couldn't suppress a grin for his enthusiasm. "That's very true. People need the right tools in order to do their jobs to the best of their ability."

"Let's get a move on, Andy. You can't get much work done if you sit and jaw half the day away." Pops headed toward the back door. Andy finished a gulp of his milk and wiped his "moustache" on his shirt sleeve as he was already on the older man's boot heels. He pulled his hat down on his head as Pops did his.

The screen door of the back porch clanged behind the pair. That left the three of them seated at the table. Gray was concentrating on his coffee cup. Thomas had leaned back against the wooden slats of his chair, arms folded in a thoughtful pose across his chest. Something was going on. She was well-schooled in body language. And that snake of dread was slowly crawling up the back of her neck. It had been her warning signal for years.

"I don't want to interrupt your business discussion, so I'll just take my plate into the…"

"This involves you, Jamie. You need to hear what Gray has to say." Thomas's words sank what was left of the balloon of hope that had risen in her heart with the morning sun. Immediately, with automatic precision, she felt the walls of defense clang into place throughout her body. The smile was gone. She looked from Thomas to the sheriff and then waited. Whatever she thought was coming, would prove to be nothing she could prepare for at all.

"Gray didn't just stop by because he was in the neighborhood. He brought some news." Thomas sat forward in his chair, long arms coming to rest before him on the table, his voice matter of fact. He could have been discussing the weather forecast for all the warmth she detected. There was a pause as if he were trying to put forward the best words.

She could never sit still and let trouble hit her without meeting it head-on. Jamie turned her steady gaze on the lawman who was looking back at her, in a quiet, assessing manner. She was used to that facade. There had been many lawmen with much the same countenance looking at her over the years. In this case, there was an underlying river of sympathy? Contrition? And Jamie felt the muscles throughout her body tense.

"I've never been one to play guessing games. I'd appreciate you both just laying whatever it is out on the table."

"I was asked to do some checking a couple of weeks ago…just a basic background run," Gray began.

Jamie stopped him. "Who asked you to do that?" Her gaze was drawn to Thomas.

"I did." He met her steady gaze with his own. She couldn't read what was shuttered away from her. The man who had held her and said such magic words in the moonlight bore little resemblance to the all-business rancher across from her now. Somewhere over the last hour or so, they had become employer/employee again. *So be it.*

"I would have thought that my being an employee of the hospital and having already passed a few background checks would have been sufficient, but I suppose I can understand your reticence at the time. After all, you wouldn't want just anyone coming into your home and being around your family." There, she had absolved him. What else would there be for them to discuss? Her attention went back to the sheriff.

"I came across some information…involving a period in your life that I'm sure you don't like to have brought up. I had just begun to share it with Thomas when Andy came in for breakfast. We changed the subject."

There it was. The dragon had not gone dormant, never to surface again. It was just waiting for the moment when her guard had gone all the way down. And now the old anger began to rise; it tasted like poison in her mouth. Jamie pushed away the plate of food in front of her. She had opened herself to trusting and believing in possibilities. Her defense mechanism kicked in and she took control of the offense.

She faced demons a long time ago. They weren't going to win this time. She would lay it all out for Thomas. "And you found out that my stepfather killed my mother by beating and kicking her to death while I hid under a table in the corner and watched him do it. Then I spent six years of my life from age ten to sixteen in foster care while I was pushed and pulled by lawyers until the day came I stood in a courtroom and testified against that monster. I watched him be taken to prison for the rest of his life, but he deserved worse. Except the jury couldn't quite understand how a woman could stay with a man who beat her at least once a day, starved her and her child just for the laughs, and threatened to do more to me. So much so that I hid under my bed instead of slept in it, because I had a baseball bat that I found in an alley one day and kept it close if he did come into my room when my mother wasn't there to protect me. I think that's what you found, correct? I am a survivor of child abuse. I was a murder witness. And I grew up in the foster system. I put it all behind me and fought to keep it there. I believe I survived instead of being a victim. And I've been a productive member of society since that time. I'm a damn good nurse. And…"

Thomas stopped her. "You aren't on trial here, Jamie. That was never meant to be the point. I asked Gray to do me a favor in the very beginning of your stay with us. Yes, I had the interest of my family in mind, but not for the reasons you seem to think. And as things progressed and I began to know the real you, I hadn't given it much thought until Gray came here this morning with his report. When you hear him out, which won't be easy, maybe you'll understand better why we're even discussing this now. But we need to let you know what news he has found."

There was pure concern in his eyes now as he looked across at her, and she felt a shiver of something run down her spine. Or was it pity? What more could there possibly be? Her attention went back to the lawman.

"In finding all of this, I had a couple of questions, so I called the district attorney's office in Houston. They shared some of the particulars that you just did. However, they've been remiss. They screwed up royally...to put it mildly. Vital information seemed to have fallen through some big cracks in the judicial system. They blamed it on lack of adequate funding to hire the staff to keep up with the changes in the prison system, but it was their mistakes that kept information from being given to you in a timely manner."

"Please tell me that the monster died in prison in some random act of prison violence. I used to pray for that as a teenager. That might not mesh with my nursing oath, but there are special circumstances to every rule."

"It would be easier that way, I suppose. And as a lawman, I took an oath, also. But there are those people who do push our civilized law-abiding buttons. And that's why what I need to tell you now is very hard to deliver. I'm just going to put it out there." He paused and then he continued in that matter-of-fact way she had expected from people in his profession.

"Garrett Dunn was granted a release due to overcrowding and a snafu in the sentencing materials. He's been out of prison for almost two months. He was warned to stay far away from you or any of the other witnesses in his trial due to a pending review of his case. He comes near you, he's back behind bars for good. They don't think he'll be that stupid. But you should have been warned ahead of time."

Jamie felt the blood drain from her body to an invisible pool on the floor. Every ounce of self-preservation seemed to go with it. The feeling of being "free" from the monster had been a sham. He was still out there in the darkness. He could have shown himself to her at any time or place. She heard his last words growled to her as she left the witness stand and the prosecutor had tried to stand between her and where Garrett sat with that deadly look in his black eyes. "You'll pay, you little bitch. Just like your mother."

The sense of security she had begun to ease into and live her adult life with had all been a lie. She had never been safe. He would come for her, and in that minute, the old need to flee was back. The need to protect herself kicked in. But another came along with it. If she wasn't safe, then no one around her would be, either. Nothing would stop the monster that Garrett Dunn was. They had no idea, but she did. Jamie stood. Both men did as well.

"I need to pack. I need to get back to my house. Thank you for letting me know what's going on. It naturally impacts what I need to do now." She turned to leave, but Thomas was fast and his hand on her arm forestalled her.

"We need to talk…Gray and I. But you and I also need to clear up some things before you do whatever you believe you need to do now. Give me some time. Meet me in my office in an hour? Promise me that much. You're not alone in this, Jamie. You'll be safer here than anyplace else, but we'll talk about that after I take care of some things with the hands and with Gray."

She owed him that much. If he hadn't been protecting his family and had a simple background check done, then she wouldn't know the danger that was headed in her direction now. Forearmed was forewarned. She had learned that the hard way. Jamie nodded.

Glancing at Gray, she tried to manage a poor semblance of a smile. "Thanks for the heads-up. I appreciate it."

He put out his hand and she accepted the handshake, but he did not release it. Instead he used it to underpin his next words along with a steady gaze. "I'd tell you not to worry, but I think you'll still do plenty of that. It's ingrained in your DNA and I recognize that. But just know that my department now has your back. Every pair of eyes is on the lookout for any sign of that man. His photo has been distributed not only in this county but all those around us. Hopefully, he is getting as far from Texas as possible while he can. But we're just a phone call away day or night. And," he produced a small white card from his chest pocket and handed it over to her, "this has my office and my cell numbers. You can reach me 24/7. Remember that."

Jamie felt a rush of emotion and knew she couldn't let them see the tears that weren't far away. She nodded her thanks and left the room.

"You put up a good front for her, but you don't buy most of what you just said about that scum, do you?" Thomas kept his voice low as he turned to face Gray. "Do you think he's coming here?"

Gray shook his head. "I wish I could be sure. From the reports I read, he isn't known for being the brightest lightbulb in the room. And his prison resume was pretty bad. I can't fathom how any idiot could have even given a second thought to releasing an animal like him into society. It was system failure, and those cracks can be awfully deep if someone isn't watching. This isn't the first time I've seen a miscarriage of justice like this one. But this happens to be my county and close to those I care about, so the walls have already gone up. It isn't just the local law enforcement that's involved. What are you thinking? I've known you long enough to know that your brain has been full throttle for the last few minutes."

Thomas nodded. "Let's step out on the back porch." Gray followed. They were out of possible earshot of anyone. "I don't think Jamie is going to submit to being locked up in one of your cells, which is where I would like to keep her until this is all worked out. It isn't smart for her to go home and be alone, although that's her flight response right now.

The next best thing is that I put up an invisible barrier as best as I can…with or without her cooperation. And I have a feeling she won't like it."

"I have a feeling you're right about that. I know you feel strongly about taking care of the people who work for you, but…"

"It's a lot more than that, and I think you figured that out before I did. Let's cut out the pretense on that one. She's a lot more than a temporary employee. And as such, I know I can count on you to be all in with my plans."

"You know you can count me in. As long as it doesn't cross the line, and you know what I mean."

Thomas gave a nod. "In other words, don't ask you to bring a shovel to dig any holes?"

Gray grimaced and Thomas gave a slight shrug. "Got to take a joke once in a while, Gray. My dad always said that the worst medicine goes down with the sweetest of intent…or some such pearl of wisdom. I want this nightmare over and done for Jamie's sake. And for the rest of us, too."

"Then let's put our heads together."

Run. The word was shouting throughout her brain. But where? What if Gray was right and Garrett would be a fool to come in her direction, even if he could locate her? People were already on the lookout for him. If she ran…where would it stop?

The one truth she did know was that she couldn't allow Thomas to try and talk her into remaining on the ranch. If Dunn did find her...and he came looking for her and found Thomas or Andy or Pops or any of the others she had come to care about first? That would be her greatest fear, unwittingly bringing a monster into their lives. They had no idea what he was capable of doing. He was insane and a killer. He hated her for telling the truth and putting him behind bars where he should never have been set free from.

No, it was her decision. Her life. And she would leave before anyone could talk her into anything else. She had her home. She had her job. And somehow she would stay safe until she could figure out a better plan. Jamie began opening drawers and closets and throwing clothes into her suitcase without much thought to neatness. She needed to get to her car and leave before Thomas came back to the house. The last thing she did was to scribble a hasty note that she left in the center of the kitchen table with his name at the top. There was so much she wanted to say but too little time.

> *My leaving is best for everyone's safety. This is my problem and no one else's. I don't want anyone else hurt. Please understand and stay away. Jamie*

She did not write the word she wanted to... *love*. She felt it. She whispered it. But she could not write it. Love could have no place in her reality.

Chapter Fourteen

IT WAS CLOSER to a full hour before Thomas entered the house again. He raced up the stairs expecting to find Jamie packing. But what he found sent his heart plummeting to the floor. The room was empty and so was the closet. He retraced his steps and crossed into the kitchen. His gaze lit on the piece of paper. Fingers grabbed it up and his eyes scanned the meager message...once and then once more. His heart sought denial while his brain screamed the reality. She was gone. She fled to keep them safe. And she was alone.

He grabbed his phone from his pocket and hit the speed dial for Gray. The sheriff answered on the third ring.

"Jamie left. There's a note. She's afraid of staying here and putting us in danger."

"I'm turning around and will be back there in under five minutes. We can formulate a plan. Don't go anywhere." The line clicked off.

Thomas knew for only the second time in his life what it felt like to be helpless and unsure of what to do. He hated that feeling. He dialed Jamie's number and wasn't surprised when she didn't answer. He begged her to call him when her voice mail came on. His next call was to Pops. He didn't have time for specifics, but he needed him to not make any other stops in town and to come back to the ranch. They needed to have a meeting, and when he came through the main gate, he needed to close it. That was enough to shock Pops into silence for a few moments. They very rarely closed those gates. Pops indicated he would handle it and the call ended.

The sound of a fast-approaching vehicle brought Thomas out onto the back porch. Gray pulled into the driveway and cut his engine. His long strides carried him to stand on the porch in just a few moments. "I'm sorry she left. Did she explain why she felt she had to leave?"

"She was gone when I got back to the house after you and I parted at the stables after talking to Daniel and the men. This was on the table. And she isn't answering my calls to her cell."

Gray took the paper and read the brief words. He shook his head. "I know you're upset and wanting to keep her safe. But you can't lock her away here if she doesn't want to stay. There is a good chance that this man is headed as far away from Texas as he can get. We'll operate under that assumption until we know different."

THE LITTLE YELLOW house with its white trim and white

shutters looked a bit forlorn to her as she pulled into the driveway. Or maybe that was just her imagination and her mood coloring the moment. The grass was due for a trim, and she knew that her neighbor's nephew was earning his money keeping it in shape. It would be due again to have a mowing this weekend. She switched off the engine and unbuckled her seat belt.

She opened the mailbox beside the front door and took out a handful of mail…mostly junk mail as she paid most of her bills automatically online each month. There were a couple of letters from nurse friends from the hospital in Dallas, and she would read them later. Fitting the key into the lock, she stepped inside. The air was still; she needed to turn up the air-conditioning and get the air circulating. She walked into the hallway, set the temperature, and switched the unit to on. The faint humming began.

Moving back to the living room, she noted there was a fine coating of dust on much of the furniture, and she would need to do some cleaning of that in each room. It would help keep her mind centered on other things besides the animal that was on the loose. She double-checked that the front door dead bolt was in place. Jamie moved next to the kitchen.

Walking into the kitchen, she noted that the pantry door was ajar a bit. She always kept it shut. Then she turned toward the sink area; that's when the hair along the back of her neck stood straight on end. Her eyes rested on a lone glass sitting next to the sink. Then things went into high gear yet felt like slow motion at the same time.

Garrett Dunn wasn't outside of Texas. He was grabbing her arm and twisting it behind her back, the other arm with the knife in hand was held against the flesh of her neck. There was pain in her arm and the knife was already cutting her skin. The man looked totally different from the last time she had seen him, in the courtroom when she had told the judge and jury what he had done to her mother. They had sentenced him to life with no parole. He had promised to get her, and he was keeping that promise. Her life was about to end. There was a flash of Thomas through her mind…and Andy. At least this wouldn't happen at the ranch.

And he'd get away with it all. He had totally changed his outward appearance…or maybe the years behind bars had done that. Either way, he was still the monster she knew him to be. His black hair was gone, his head shaved bald. He had gotten some ill-fitting clothing, a mechanics coverall. If he were seen on the street, a passerby would think he was a hard-working mechanic on his lunch hour. No one would know a monster was in their midst.

"Did you miss me? I told you I'd find you and you'd pay. Almost twenty years I sat in that cell thinking of this moment, and then those idiots played right into my hands. I have to hand it to you, you were a little hard to track, but thanks to your chatty friend at that hospital in Dallas, it was child's play getting your address in this little hayseed town.

But we're wasting time. I can't have cops spoiling my fun. I dreamed every night about the pain I'm going to give you. You'll beg for the end by the time I finish. Now let's move out to the garage. My truck's in there. I've been sitting in this place for the last three days waiting on you. Keep your mouth shut or I'll start carving into you right now."

He pulled her toward the back door. Jamie kept her mind on one thing. She needed some way to inflict pain, to fight back. She wasn't going to make it easy on him. She had read books on self-defense, and she knew she didn't have the body strength to overpower him, but she had brains. As long as she didn't allow panic to take over and short-circuit her brain, she might have a chance…*might.* She spied the little red bottle opener on the side of the refrigerator. When he went to open the door, she quickly pulled the opposite direction and it threw him off-balance for just a couple of seconds, but it was enough. Her hand managed to grab the object and she kept it tight in her palm. For her transgression, he literally dislocated her shoulder. The pain almost made her pass out…almost. The fear kept her brain moving.

"I've got a gun in my other pocket, so if you think about getting someone's attention like that little old lady next door, she'll be collateral damage. Got it?"

Jamie said nothing. The pain was growing worse, so she had to concentrate and breathe through it. He walked them both out to the garage, and they entered through the side door. There was an older model pickup that had seen better days. For a moment, she thought she heard the blare of a siren in the distance.

He opened the passenger door and shoved her inside. Then he was beside her and the engine started. He pulled away from the house, and she was able to see her car, but no one was around it.

"Where are we going?"

"Shut up. We're going to find a nice quiet place where you can scream your head off and no one will hear…except maybe the coyotes, but they can have what's left of you."

"Why do this? You could be far away by now…even in another country. Staying here only makes it easier for them to throw you back in prison. They'll give you the death sentence this time. You know that."

"This is worth it. But I won't be put back into a cell. Not over you. You should have kept your mouth shut. You and that mother of yours were always trouble."

Jamie realized that he was getting even more agitated. He wasn't going to listen to anything she said. He was way past being reasoned with. Her only hope was to not allow him to take her out of town, away from people. Because once he isolated her, there would be no hope. She needed to take matters into her own hands. If she was going to go down, she would decide when and how.

But she needed to put an end to him. He wasn't familiar with Faris. He had no idea that he would be going through the middle of town. He would pass the courthouse and there would be people around. But that was bad, too. Too many people that might get hurt. She fought down the panic that threatened to let loose again. *Thomas... Gray... Someone.* She was on her own. She had been that way since the day her mother was killed. It was up to her to be a victim or a survivor. She made her decision.

"AND IF HE isn't in Georgia? I'm going to have the men sit on her house in town, and..."

"Whoa!" Gray held up a hand. "That is not what you're going to do. That might have been the solution if she were here on your land. But in town, she is under law enforcement's watch. My deputies will take on that responsibility, not you or your men. Understood?"

Thomas remained silent. Then he slowly nodded. "I hear you."

"Don't give me that. I want you to say, yes, Gray, I understand and I will not interfere. Say it."

"We're wasting time."

"No, I'm not. I called my chief deputy on the way back here. I have him heading over to her house and I'll be going that way after I make certain you understand what I..." He cut off his sentence and looked at the phone in his other hand. He frowned. "What's up?" He spoke to the caller. Then his demeanor changed; his body tensed. Thomas felt a bad feeling begin in the pit of his stomach.

"I'll meet you there. Roll the others and the crime scene team. No comments to anyone at this time."

The sheriff's gaze met Thomas's. "Jamie's neighbor called the office. She saw Jamie pull into her driveway. A few minutes later, she was at her kitchen window and she saw some man pulling Jamie toward the garage. She said Jamie looked like she didn't want to go with him. Then a pickup left the house driving at a reckless speed down the street. My deputies are on the way."

"He's here. He was waiting for her." Thomas was moving toward his truck.

"In my vehicle," Gray yelled at him. "We'll get there faster."

Lights flashing, siren wailing, and Thomas's heart was beating louder than any of it. At least that's how it seemed to him as Gray's vehicle seemed to be going in slow motion even though he could see the speedometer was pushing close to three digits. His brain was fighting to keep all the images out of it. But his imagination wasn't stopping. The longer the animal named Dunn had Jamie in his clutches, the more his brain was on overdrive.

There were bits and pieces of conversation between Gray and his personnel, but Thomas only heard Jamie's voice in his brain as he replayed the too-short time they spent together over the last several weeks. He needed more time. He needed to say so many things to her.

"Don't let your mind go to places it doesn't need to be. Stick to the facts we have. We'll find her. He isn't getting out of this county."

Thomas nodded. Words were in short supply at the moment.

Chapter Fifteen

"HE WASN'T WORRIED about fingerprints. They're all over Jamie's house. And the police dog tracked them outside the house to the garage. The next-door neighbor gave a good description of the truck, and it's already out on the airwaves. People are searching the town and all roads in and out." Gray returned to where Thomas was standing beside the vehicle while Gray had gone inside with his men and gotten an update on what had been found. The report didn't make Thomas feel any better.

About that time a deputy came out of the house and walked to where they stood. "We have eyes on the vehicle moving through the downtown area. You want us to stop it now?"

"No. It could be dangerous pulling him over with so many people in the area. Follow as discreetly as you can and keep it in your sights. Let's box him in but in a spot of our choosing. I'm headed that way. Load up, Thomas." The pair set off with lights flashing.

Thomas's brain was firing on too many levels. He had to fight to keep the worst thoughts from his mind. All he could do was keep begging in silence to whatever higher being would listen. *Let her be okay. Let her come home.*

Gray worked the radio, giving orders where he wanted roadblocks set up.

"He doesn't know we have a description of his vehicle, so he's taking it easy and not attracting attention. But that won't last if he knows he's being tailed. He'll hit the gas and run for it. We need him away from populated areas of town."

Thomas nodded in response to Gray's words. "Then you need to hit that gas pedal of yours and get us there before that happens."

"Hang in there. Remember, Jamie is a very smart lady."

"If he gets out of town, there are a hundred oil field roads and dirt tracks he could get lost down. We'd never find them. I should have gone right after her this morning when I found the note. I would have been right behind her at the house. I could have…"

Gray shook his head. "Knock it off. You could have walked into an ambush. We'll find Jamie. And you'll get the chance to tell her how you feel about her."

Thomas didn't respond…not out loud. *A chance. One more chance.* How many chances can someone have to make things right?

"Two more lights and then we'll shake the dust of this town. I found us a nice, quiet little spot away from any people. We don't want to be disturbed. I've got a lot of plans for us. Nineteen years is a long time to plan something."

Garrett Dunn was talking more to himself than to her. Jamie realized that he had spiraled way past any chance of reason or pleading. Time was running out. They would soon leave the main part of town and head out toward the open ranchland. There were two roads he might choose. She tried to map out in her brain where there might be chances for her to try to get away. She had already decided that either way involved danger and perhaps serious physical injuries to herself. But if she did nothing, the only option looking at her was death at his hands. While she could, she would control her own destiny.

Keeping her head down as he ordered, she tried to cast glances out the window beside her. The pain in her shoulder and arm was past the point of intense, and yet she used it to fuel her determination.

The truck was old, no side mirror on her side. Hopefully, when she could grab for the door lever beside her, the popup lock would be in working order. They were passing the square. She could see people going about their usual daily errands, never knowing the monster passing them. They couldn't know she needed help. Where was help? Then the realization would quickly follow that it was up to her to do something.

The truck turned to the left, and she knew there were only a handful of blocks left. The time was ticking too fast. Her fingers curled around the bottle opener, finding the end with the sharp triangular metal. She needed speed and no hesitancy. When you hesitated, you got hurt. She remembered the kind policewoman telling her that one day while they waited outside the courtroom. Jamie had asked her how a person could protect themselves if they were too young to have access to a gun. The woman had shared some of her knowledge with her. It wasn't going to be a gun that was the best protector. It was a person's brain. She had remembered that. She had to trust in that.

Another block there was construction ahead. She had passed it many times on her way to the hospital. They were putting in large drainage pipes and the mounds of dirt had been growing. Would they still be there? Maybe they would break her fall…if she got that far. Once she got outside the truck, she needed to be able to get up and run. What if she couldn't? Jamie shoved that thought away. *Don't build roadblocks.*

He had to slow the truck considerably to go around the barricades. One more turn…deep breath…only chance. There was an unexpected bump, and it served to move her while his attention was on the road. Her arm came up in an arc of motion and she felt the metal hit bone; there was an animal-like howl that filled the cab of the truck. The hands on the wheel tightened, and his foot pushed the gas pedal full throttle in the sudden pain of the unexpected attack.

Jamie was on autopilot. Her good shoulder went into the door beside her. Her free hand pulled up on the lever. With gritted teeth, she felt the door swing open, and then rushing air and space met her. It was much the same feeling as the moment she stepped off the platform when her unit had talked her into going bungy jumping in their team building exercises last spring. Only there was no pull back from the brink of hitting the ground this time. But luck was with her, and a four-foot mound of dirt, weeds, and pea gravel caught the full impact of her flying body. The momentum sent her rolling down the other side into a newly dug ditch.

In the distance, there was a grinding of an engine motor and then a tremendous explosion that shook the ground around her. For a brief moment, she associated it with her body hitting the earth. Then she tried to take a breath into her lungs and there was none.

THOMAS AND GRAY saw the billow of smoke rising over the tree line while they were still three blocks away. A couple of units with lights flashing and sirens blaring raced ahead of them. They turned a corner and were lost to sight. Thomas felt his insides turn inside out as the thought of what might be around the corner ahead of them set in. When they came to a flying halt behind the firetrucks where firemen were pulling hoses and opening hydrants, he slid out of the vehicle and began to run toward the flames. Gray and another officer grabbed him and held him in check.

"Let them do their jobs." Gray's voice sounded hollow to Thomas's ears. Gray's stone-faced countenance registered. *He knows it's too late. It is too late.* His knees lost their strength and without the two men holding him between them, he would have sunk to the ground in that moment.

Jamie. His heart felt hollow and gutted. He had left things too late. He needed her to know how he felt, and he had waited too long.

The incessant barking of orders from a small knot of paramedics and other law enforcement filtered into his thoughts. Gray looked behind them to some point in the distance. "Is that…what the…they've found something on the other side of the ditch. Check it out, Officer Scott." He nodded to the deputy on the other side of Thomas. The man left in a hurry.

Thomas shut his eyes against the scene where the smoke had turned to white plumes from the black billows. He felt Gray tense beside him. Thomas followed his gaze and saw the deputy waving his arms and pointing. Others were moving in that direction, along with an ambulance.

There were voices Thomas couldn't make out coming across the radio attached to Gray's shoulder strap. But Gray was understanding them. He began to nod his head. He looked at Thomas and there was a change of expression. "She wasn't in there…in the truck. She must have jumped before he hit the dump truck full on. EMS has her and they're heading to the emergency room. Understand?"

Thomas heard the words shouting over and over inside his brain. He began to run toward the group of men and stopped only when the gurney with the body covered in a white blanket emerged, moving quickly toward the back of the waiting ambulance. He had to see her for himself. Gray made an opening between two firemen and Thomas saw the brown hair, the flash of purple material of the blouse she had been wearing that morning at breakfast. There were mud streaks and blood smears across her forehead and down her cheek. She looked so pale. His heart had climbed to the top of the mountain of hope and then it nosedived as he saw the closed eyes and the way the EMTs were moving.

"Let them take care of her, Thomas," Gray said, pulling him back when he would have tried to climb inside. "We'll meet them at the hospital." Thomas nodded. That was about all he was capable of; he was strictly on autopilot. He was glad that Gray didn't try to offer platitudes and empty promises as they sped after the ambulance. All his mind could handle was keeping his gaze locked on the red and white vehicle ahead of them. Jamie was there, and she could be gone at any moment. No one had offered any guarantee of anything. But as long as she moved, he would follow.

Gray shook his head. "Whatever she managed to do, Jamie saved herself. I need to call Dottie and Pops when we get to the hospital and let them know what is going on. You'll want to speak to Andy when you think the time is right."

As they pulled into a parking space reserved for law enforcement in the ER area, the crew was already unloading Jamie, and a group of doctors and nurses stood ready to receive her. The mass moved inside, and Thomas and Gray were right behind them. Then doors shut and Thomas was left to stare at their dull grayness with their warning signs of *No Admittance* attached to them. He never got to speak to Jamie. He paced like a caged lion, not pausing and with his gaze glued to the doors.

At some point Pops arrived. He and Gray kept a conversation going, but Thomas couldn't keep his mind on it. Horses, cattle prices, rodeo schedules…nothing measured against the need to have someone tell him if the woman he loved was still alive. If there would be another chance. He knew Pops was keeping Dottie and the ranch in the loop with what little information there was to share at the moment. Dottie was plying Andy with his favorite foods and even an hour in the pool was in the cards, but Andy wanted to know where Jamie was and when she'd be back. As his backup, he wanted to talk to his dad. Thomas placed the call as soon as Pops relayed the message.

"Hi, Dad! Is Jamie with you? I'm helping Miss Dottie with some chocolate chip cookies. And she said I can go swimming later. Will you and Jamie be here to go swimming, too?"

Thomas batted moisture out of the corners of his eyes. His son loved Jamie before any of them had wised up enough to follow suit. And now he might have to be the one to tell him that she might not stay with them. He couldn't bring himself to say much more. "You and Jasper help Dottie this afternoon and look after things at the ranch for me. I'll be home later and then I'll tell you what is keeping Jamie busy today. You take care of things until I get there, okay? Love you. Bye, son."

Maybe he was being a coward. But he knew that he would need to be with Andy when he found out the truth. The little boy could stay in his world where all was good, and Jamie would be home soon. Thomas had no idea how long this could go on and what lay ahead of them before the sun set on the day. He heard Gray talking on his phone in quiet tones to Tori.

She'd fill in his brothers. They knew how to get through tragedies…but he didn't want to add another one to the list. The doors swished open behind him, and he heard his name. Gray stood up and so did Pops. His breath caught in his chest. Thomas squared his shoulders ready for the hit, as he turned to face Dr. Cuesta and the other doctor standing beside him.

"That is one lucky lady. And a tough one, too." The robed man began with those words. Positive words…that much registered in Thomas's brain. "Besides taking care of the superficial cuts and scrapes on her and the dislocated shoulder, we took a lot of X-rays, did some scans, and other tests." Dr. Cuesta nodded his head toward the doctor beside him. "While we still have a couple to read when they're ready, I think Dr. Lamb, head of our neurosurgery team and I can agree that she managed to survive what could have been far worse. Barring any surprises in the rest of the tests, I expect her to be in the hospital for a few days, mostly for observation and to allow some bruised parts to begin healing. There are some stitches and dressings. And for the next day or so, she'll be on pain meds. The best thing is to allow her to rest and get a good start on the healing process."

"Can I see her right now?" Thomas spoke up.

"I know we need to give the sheriff a couple of minutes with her, then the pain meds will kick in. Tomorrow morning should be soon enough for anyone else...and that's up to the patient. Let her rest, son." The doctor met his gaze with one tinged with compassion. "Be thankful she has survived and will be back on her feet sooner than later. We just need to give her time to heal."

"I'll let her know you're here," Gray said, moving to follow the two men through the double doors. Pops stepped up beside Thomas.

"One of the hands followed me into town as I drove your truck in for you. It's in the lot outside." He handed over the key ring. "I'll head on back to the ranch. I take it that you'll not be leaving right now," Pops said. It wasn't a question.

"No, I'm staying here unless they toss me out. Tell Dottie she's appreciated more than I can tell her."

"She knows all that. But I'll deliver the message. You know where I'll be if you need me." Thomas watched the older man walk down the hall. Only then did he find he could take in a breath without holding it. The news was better than he had any right to hope. It could have been far worse. But he knew that until the moment came when Jamie could leave the hospital and go back to her regular routine, he wouldn't know relief. Life always held a few surprises when a person least expected them.

Look at yesterday afternoon. He had made up his mind on the ride into town. Leaving his meeting earlier than planned, he had stopped into Foxworth's Jewelry. He had handed over his mother's engagement ring and chosen a design to modernize it and added a larger center stone. A cluster of diamonds would surround a perfect solitaire. It would shine with brilliance, reminding him of how the sunlight sparked off the highlights in her hair when Jamie allowed it to hang free and the wind caught and played through it. Or maybe it would remind him of the brightness of her smile when something pleased her, and she let herself enjoy the moment. The ring would be waiting for the right moment. *Just in case.*

He had been working out the details in his mind on the words he wanted to say to Jamie. They needed to be just right. But then this morning came along and his whole life slid into a dark nightmare. The clock ticked on the nearby wall. Thomas ran another hand over his face and through the hair on his head. Somewhere, he had lost his hat along the way. That was the least of his priorities. The door opened and Gray stood there, motioning for him to come inside, in a covert movement of his hand. Thomas didn't need a second invite.

"Stay quiet and follow me. I shouldn't be doing this. We'll both get kicked out if that head nurse sees us." The man was his entrance to wherever Jamie was, so Thomas was stuck to him like a fly on sticky paper. Gray pushed open the third door on the right and motioned him inside. "She comes in and out of the meds. I'll stand outside the door and act like I'm making a phone call. If I say we need to leave, then move it...no questions asked." He slipped back out into the hallway and Thomas's gaze homed in on the form in the bed. The beeps and machines and tubes were forced into the background as he moved to her side. His hand closed over one of hers, lying so still on top of the blanket.

Making contact with her sent a wave of incredible calm washing over and through him. He leaned down to whisper next to her ear. "Jamie. It's me, Thomas. I'm right here. Do you hear me?"

A soft frown creased her forehead. It disappeared and her eyes stayed closed. "Can you look at me for just a second? I want to say something before they throw me out. Please, Jamie. Open your eyes for me if you can."

The long lashes fluttered a time or two on her cheeks.

Then he saw the deep chocolate orbs peek from beneath them in his direction. She was there with him! *Hold it together, cowboy.*

"I can't stay long, but I want you to hear the words. Everything else we can talk about later when you feel better. I love you, Jamie Westmoreland. From the very first moment. And I will until my last breath. I hope you can hear that. I'll remind you every day."

"Pssst! Move it, the head nurse is on the floor and heading this way." Gray's voice was as loud a whisper as he could chance as he stuck his head in the doorway.

Thomas nodded, his gaze not leaving Jamie. "I have to leave, but I'll be back. Did you hear me?" The eyes blinked slowly. Then they stayed closed. Thomas placed a swift kiss on her forehead and moved away. Gray's hand on his shoulder hurried his steps out of the room and down the hall. They could feel the glare of the nurse's eyes boring into their backs. Her steps increased behind them. They did not look back. And they didn't stop until the gray doors closed behind them.

"I OWE YOU big-time for that," Thomas said, as they reached their vehicles.

"I figure you'd do the same for me if the boots were on the other feet. This way you'll get some sleep tonight and be of use to the rest of us tomorrow."

"Did you get to talk to her about anything that happened?"

"Enough. She is one tough lady and used her brains. That's what saved her. As the days go by, we'll be busy tying up loose ends and doing all the crossing of t's and dotting of i's to put the story of Garrett Dunn and this whole mess of him being let out and finding Jamie behind us. We'll make certain that enough heat is turned up that those cracks in the system are cemented over for good. The important part is that Jamie is done with him. He can never hurt her or anyone else."

"We have to be thankful that the road construction was going on. It stopped him or he might have gotten away."

Gray shook his head. "That did help matters in stopping him. Actually, Jamie used them. By using her wits and guts, she took care of the situation. She chose the spot and with a ridiculous can opener she grabbed from her refrigerator door, she managed to inflict a lot of pain and damage to his face. That caused him to swerve toward the dump truck, and she opened her door and jumped…landing on top of a lot of loose dirt piled there. Someone was looking out for her. But she was determined that she was going to stop him before he could get out into the oil fields. He came here to kill her. He made sure he described his plan to her as they drove, inflicting more emotional wounds. I'll let you read the completed report when it's done…if you want to do so. But remember, it's done. He'll just be a bad memory and that will hopefully fade in time. Jamie's still here. Andy and everyone else is okay and that is what matters."

"Yes, that is *all* that matters. I won't forget that." Thomas spoke the words as they were etched into his heart. He tossed a look over at the sheriff. "And I might have to amend my opinion about my sister being too good for you. It might be that *you're* too good for *her*. But as I say, I *might* have to rethink things. Tomorrow could always change my mind again."

Chapter Sixteen

"I WISH YOU'D let me come by and help you when you get home tomorrow. At least until you get settled in." Dottie was doing her best to change Jamie's mind. But it was falling on deaf ears.

"Dottie, you are an angel and have been such a good friend to me. And you're certainly welcome to stop by and visit…after I get settled into things. But I will have home visits from my physical therapist and a home care nurse for a few hours each day for the next couple of weeks. I need to do this on my own. I hope you can understand how important that is to me. The counselor that I've begun to visit with here in the hospital will also be there to support my decision. I had to fight for quite some time to get control of my life the first time Garrett Dunn was in my life. Now, I must do it again. No one can do that for me."

"I understand. I do. But you can't fault those of us who have come to love you. We want only the best for you. I'm glad that you're letting Andy come see you today. If he asks once, he asks a hundred times between sunup and sundown when he can come visit." She paused and then made her next remark. "Of course, his dad isn't much better. He just likes to bite people's heads off along the way. But he'll give you space if that's what you say you need. Doesn't mean that he likes it…not one little bit."

Jamie paused in folding her nightgowns and placing them in the open overnight bag on her bed. "I know it's been hard on a lot of people. I hate that my past touched on the people I care about here. When I think how Andy might have been hurt, I just can't describe what I feel. That's why I left the ranch the way I did that day. I was afraid Dunn would come to the ranch and then there's no telling who he might have hurt…because of me. I know that Thomas can't understand all of this. But I know what I need in order to get back to my life, and people need to trust that."

There was a light knock and Pops stuck his head in the room. "I've got a cowboy out here looking for Nurse Jamie. Looks like we're bending the rules again." He finished with a wink.

"What else are rules meant for?" Jamie responded with a grin. "He best come inside then."

The door pushed open and in rushed a miniature cowhand, his hat on his head and his boots clacking on the polished floor. His eyes lit up like huge blue beacons when he spied Jamie standing there. Three steps and he was folded inside her arms in a huge bear hug, his arms locking around her waist. Her eyes misted over.

"Dottie, lets you and me go get a cup of coffee. We'll be

back in two shakes." The woman nodded.

"We'll be right back."

Jamie sat down on the edge of the bed and helped Andy to climb up in a similar position. She held his hand in hers. "You seem to have grown a foot in these six days. How's Jasper?"

"Jasper's okay. He's taking care of things like he always does. He misses you, too. I can tell."

"And how about you?"

He shook his head and looked up at her with a solemn gaze. "I missed you a whole lot, but my dad said we needed to do whatever we could to help you get better faster. And you didn't want anyone to come to the hospital, so we had to wait. But I got to come see you now. I just wish you were coming home with us today."

"I know. It's hard to understand, I guess. But I need to go back to my own house and to a routine that makes sense for me and my job at the hospital, too. Your dad is all healed and he doesn't need a nurse any longer. But now it seems it's *my* turn to need a nurse, and I will get better, too. You and I can certainly keep in touch with phone calls. That will be good, won't it?"

"I guess so. But can you come and ride horses sometimes, too? My dad misses you a lot. He thinks I don't know that. He says we have to help you get better by doing what you need us to do. It's just that he doesn't smile or laugh very much anymore. And he goes riding a lot without me. It just isn't the same without you."

Jamie had known it would be hard to see Andy and try to make him understand, but she had no idea it would be so heartbreaking. How could she make him understand that she missed them all just as much as they missed her? And part of her wanted to be with them? How she blamed herself for bringing all of this sadness upon them? She halted her thoughts when it came to Thomas. Her heart ached beyond words when she remembered their time together…the kisses, the way he had stolen into her heart, and how he was trying his best to honor her wishes even now.

But she knew that even he couldn't be patient forever. She tried to remember if she had dreamed him coming into her room and saying he loved her. When she had mentioned it to one of the nurses that had been on duty that first night, she brushed her off with a laugh. "You know that Aggie wouldn't allow anyone onto her floor and that includes good-looking ranchers like Thomas Tremayne. No one was allowed in here while you were sleeping." She had chalked it up to being a dream and nothing more.

"Let's go, Andy," Pops said, walking into the room. "Dottie is waiting downstairs with the sheriff. He'll be right up to take you home, Miss Jamie. If you need anything at all…"

"I know," she said with a laugh. "If I need anything at all, just call and you'll come faster than a rabbit being chased by a coyote. Did I get the wording right?"

"You sure did. And I mean it. We'll be seeing you." Was that a hint of mist in the man's eye as he turned away? That touched Jamie's heart even more. Andy grabbed her in another hug, and she placed a kiss on top of his head.

"Be good. Don't be in such a hurry to grow so tall. And give Jasper an extra dog biscuit for me, okay?"

He joined Pops at the door and grinned. "I'll do it. I love you, Nurse Jamie." And then he disappeared out the door.

Those words would be held close to her heart forever. Along with the imagined ones that his father whispered in a dream. They would be part of her healing. People cared about her and she them. It was a good place to begin to forget the nightmares.

"Your designated driver is here." Gray came in with a smile on his face. "You are one popular lady from what I hear from the nurses. They say you spent part of the morning giving away the flowers that came your way."

"I couldn't make you carry all of those flowers in your sheriff's car. And why not share the flowers and have them brighten other patients' days? I know from experience how they can help a lonely or scared patient."

"Let's get your suitcase and get you set free of this place. It's a gorgeous day outside."

"I FEEL LIKE this is such an imposition to have you drive me home. I could have driven myself."

"I do get a lunch break now and then, and being the boss as you might recall, I can do what I please...most of the time," he added with a grin. Jamie marveled, not for the first time, how Tori Tremayne could keep ignoring such a hunk of a man, and one with a pure heart of gold. If she didn't know that there was even a more perfect man out there, a certain rancher with the bluest eyes in Texas, then she might get in line with the other females in Faris, who swooned when the lawman walked down the street. But her heart had found its home, and she feared it would be a forever situation.

Jamie's heartbeat had picked up as they navigated the streets and finally turned down the one leading her home. She took in the yellow and white house as they drove into the driveway and fought to keep the flashbacks tamped down. It wasn't too hard to do given the fact that there were some things that were different. The grass had been mowed and trimmed. Rose bushes had been added, along with a few more shrubs in the front flower bed. The shutters sported fresh paint. She didn't say anything as Gray was already out of the car and taking her bag from the back seat.

He stepped around and offered her the support of his arm as they went up the sidewalk. The bruising along her left side was getting easier to deal with, but it did cause her to alter the length of her steps. Her balance issues were fading and that was good. The two steps leading to her porch were done one step at a time. She took the key in her hand and fitted it into the lock. The door opened back, and she stepped through into the living room. At least she thought it was her living room.

There were bright flowerpots and a collage of flowers and green plants along the bar that separated the kitchen and living room. They sat on the coffee table, too. It was evident that the house had also undergone a deep cleaning, including carpets and draperies. She had a feeling she knew the response to her question even before she asked. Gray looked a bit uncomfortable as he set the bag down where she indicated and straightened, his smile a bit sheepish.

"Dottie might have spent some time over here. Pops, Thomas, Miguel…some of the wives of the ranch hands. And maybe an off-duty lawman…or two."

"I see. Who was the ringleader of this gang?"

"That would be the one who usually gets me into trouble—Thomas Tremayne. But no one really had to have their arms twisted or be blackmailed. It was just something we wanted to do once we heard Dottie mention that you planned to do some spiffing-up of the place. A coat of paint here and there…some plants…just a few things we could knock out in a couple of days."

"I won't make a big deal of it. Just know that it means more than I can say." She stood on tiptoe and placed a light kiss of thanks on the cheek he tilted toward her. "And is this the sort of trouble you two usually get into?"

"Well, not necessarily. I mean the last time was the day you were admitted into the hospital. I took pity on him and snuck him into your room after being warned not to allow anyone else in the room because they had given you sleep meds. But I knew that I would no more than get home and get a call to go back to the hospital to haul Thomas out of your room when he had found a way to break the house rules. The guy had suffered enough that day waiting to get news of you. So I snuck him inside and stood guard outside the door. We had to skedaddle when the shift changed; the head nurse on that shift is not someone to mess with."

Jamie took the news in and rolled it around inside her brain for a couple of minutes. "So Thomas really was inside my room that night? I thought I had dreamed that part."

"Well, you were pretty well out of it by the time I left you after taking your initial statement. But I knew that he needed to see you for himself or he'd go 'round the bend. I couldn't blame the guy. It's hard to see someone you love…someone you care so much about and all hurting, and you can't do anything to help them. I hope I didn't put my foot into my big mouth just now. I make it a policy not to get involved in the middle of anyone's personal business when it involves the heart and well…I need to shut my mouth and take my leave." He drew his hat down on his head and moved to the front door. "I put another of my cards on the refrigerator door and it has my cell number on it, in case you lost the first one. Call me any hour of the day or night."

"You're a good guy, Sheriff. Thank you for being my friend."

JAMIE UNPACKED, PUT away her things, and then could put it off no longer. She walked into the kitchen and faced the pantry door. Or at least where she thought her pantry door had been. It had been transformed into shelving with beautiful brown wood framing the new glass fronts. The same wood had been used in various ways around the kitchen, and it gave the room a whole new look. She could only stand there and shake her head. Thomas had done this for her. She knew that he had read the report of that day…all the horrid details from the time she had walked into the house until she had been taken to the hospital and Garrett Dunn's charred remains had been taken to the morgue. Thomas was trying to make it easier for her. He was giving her space. But his presence was felt just the same.

One day at a time. Time will heal all. As long as she kept repeating those words, then she'd get through the days to come. And she wanted them to come. She wanted to find her balance again, to know that there was nothing to fear lurking someplace beyond the horizon of the past. She had faced down the monster, and he had been slain. That was something she was glad to have the counselor working with her on. In her profession, she had always been one of the people working to keep patients alive. Jamie had never been one to do harm…to be responsible for another's demise. But then she hadn't sought to kill. She had sought to stay alive. When faced with the threat of her own death, she chose to fight. And she could deal with that openly.

She had finally harnessed the power of fear and turned it into a renewed strength and knowledge of what she wanted going forward. Jamie had opened to possibilities and hopes that she had not allowed to be important before. Darkness had clouded life for far too long. She craved the sunlight and what a new day would bring. And she knew that her heart had also opened itself to desires and dreams; a certain cowboy played a big part in that.

Each day, Jamie had her routine, and the bruises began to fade…inside and out. Physical therapy got her balance issues dealt with, and she felt better after each session. The news of the Tremaynes was handled by Dottie's twice a week visits with her freshly baked cinnamon rolls, or lemon bars, or some other delicious delicacy that went along with a cup of coffee and the latest news.

Andy sent her drawings from the art classes he was taking as his new school year began. Her refrigerator was covered in them. He called her with Dottie's help every other day. She knew that Trey was well on his way to winning his sixth gold belt buckle after the points began adding up after the summer of back-to-back rodeos. Truitt was in the running for bullfighter of the year accolades. Tori's bulls were bucking riders off right and left. And then there was Thomas.

Dottie always ended with him. Jamie tried to not seem overly interested or show the hunger she had for news of the man. But it was there. And she missed him more each day instead of less. Then the day came when it was time to go back to her job at the hospital. Her scrubs in place, she looked in the mirror and saw an old friend there. Yet, there had been a change. It was inside her. And it was in her priorities and the feeling that while she had gained her sense of self back, there was still a missing piece in all of it.

Then, the inevitable happened. She stopped at the post office to mail a package for one of the nurses at the hospital. Coming out of the door, she came face-to-face with Thomas, who was stepping onto the sidewalk at that moment from his pickup. They both stopped and to anyone looking on, they must have seemed like a couple of bad actors in a dark comedy. He stood still, his gaze guarded but his body language concerned and unsure. She would never have credited him with ever being uncertain about anything. Yet, there he was. Looking so tall and strong and so good. She felt an immediate desire to run into his arms. But she didn't.

He spoke across the silence first.

"Hello, Jamie. You're looking well. I see you're in uniform again. I heard Dottie mention you were back at work. That must make you happy."

"Hello, Thomas. Thank you. Yes, I'm back at the hospital. It was a bit strange at first, but now it's back to the usual routine. Dottie mentioned to me about how the family is doing so well on the rodeo circuit. That's good. And Andy keeps me fully stocked with his artwork. He has a real talent and a good eye for drawing."

"Yes, I suppose he does. He's been with Tori and the guys for the last week or so. He'll be home in a couple of days."

Why did it have to be so awkward between them? How could she bring up what happened at the hospital? Had he changed his mind? Did he wish he hadn't said those words about loving her? Maybe he had. Had it all been left too long?

"Thank you. I waited too late to say that to you." She jumped into the silent void. "What you did with my house and all of you…but I know you instigated it."

"I just wanted you to have something different, a fresh start that you needed…or at least I felt you might want. I'm just glad to know that it helped in some way."

"I know. I thank you for that, too. For giving me the space, and for understanding why I reacted the way I did. It means more than I can say."

His gaze had warmed, and she wanted nothing more than to be held in his arms once more. But she still didn't reach out. And neither did he. Silence settled again.

"I need to…"

"I just came…"

They both began talking at the same time and then stopped.

"Take care of yourself, Jamie. If you need anything, you know you can call. Maybe come out on a day off and take a ride with Andy. He'd really like that."

She summoned a smile from deep within. "Thanks. I just might take you up on that offer…of the ride. Give everyone my best. Take care, Thomas." She walked away first. She had to because she was about to dissolve into tears. The pain in her heart was too sharp. If he said anything else, she didn't hear it. And she couldn't look back.

Chapter Seventeen

"SO YOU SAW her. And you stood on the corner and just chatted." Tori sat on her horse, next to Thomas, who pretended to be watching the ranch hands pen and vaccinate the cattle. He had been working before dawn to well after sundown on the ranch. Tori and Andy had arrived the day before. He was rethinking having taken a break from working the chutes to catch up with his sister. She seemed intent on talking about Jamie.

"Nothing unusual to run into people at the post office."

"Oh, *please*. You didn't run into Molly Mason and get the lowdown on her latest arthritic problems or find out what new recipe they're going to try at the diner for Sunday lunch. You ran into the woman you are head over heels about. That hasn't changed has it?"

He shot her a quick look that told her what she could do with that idea. "No, it hasn't. Not that it's any business of yours."

"Well, it's going to have to be, I guess. You two need a lot of help."

"You don't know what you're talking about. You've been

gone for weeks now. How do you know anything?"

"I know *you*. And I know she's just as miserable as you are after I stopped and had coffee with her this morning. She's got a cute little place. She's got a great job. And she seems to be keeping all the bad stuff that happened in the past and well-behind her. Yet, she is miserable. And that's all thanks to *you*."

She exasperated him on the best of days. Thomas would have left her sitting there alone, but she had dropped the fact that she had seen Jamie just that morning. So he stayed his horse and narrowed his gaze on his sister.

"How long before you tell me what you're dying to tell me about how I screwed everything up? Because I can't figure it out. I fell for the woman. I thought I made that plain to her on more than one occasion. Then it all went to pieces, and she told people she needed time to heal and get her life back together. I can understand that. I stepped back and I left her to it. I don't know what you females want from us. Casey left because she didn't get what she wanted. I thought I did all I could with Jamie, and she still left, too."

"Wow, you are truly way off point. Let me point out your failings, big brother." She raised a gloved hand, one finger going up. At least it wasn't the middle one. "Casey and Jamie…there are no comparisons. Everyone but *you* figured out what your ex wanted by the second date. She wanted a gold ring on her finger, a baby to keep you hooked, and the keys to your bank account. You were lucky when she did leave you."

Her second finger went up next. "Along comes Jamie. She's the *real* deal. As different as night and day from Casey. Despite you being yourself, she was able to fall in love with you anyway. And yet, you still managed to blow it. You say you *showed* her. What does that mean?"

"You're too young for details, but let's say there were quite a few shared kisses. And that's all you get on that subject."

"You kissed her. Maybe a little bit more…maybe not. But I don't want to know that part. Did you say the word that leaves no doubt in a female's mind as to how you feel? The 'L' word?"

"Yes, Miss Smarty-pants. I told her I loved her in the hospital after they brought her in."

Tori looked skeptical. "You actually told her to her face? And what did she say?"

"I might have whispered the words. And no, she didn't respond. But she opened her eyes and then she closed them. They had her pretty sedated."

"You've got to be kidding me. How did I deserve such a dork for a brother? Trey needs to give you some lessons with the opposite sex. And I *never* thought I'd say that."

"I don't need lessons from any of you three."

"She probably has no memory of you being there, much less saying anything to her. How could you seriously think otherwise? Because I can tell you, that the woman I left today, would be right *here*, right *now* if she thought you truly cared. The key, you big idiot, is that the woman needs not to be on drugs or anything else when you own up to being such an idiot and needing her more than you need any other animal on this ranch. Or some such romantic nonsense. I can't figure out everything for you men. If you've got the guts, you go to her, look her in the eye, and say those words again. *I dare you.*"

"So now it's a dare?"

"And don't think that your charm is enough. She deserves it to be special. But special to *her*. That might take some thought. I don't see her as the typical moonlight and roses and a fancy place type of gal. It has to be something that will be special each time she thinks about it for the next fifty years or however long you manage to not blow it with her."

Thomas hated to admit when his little sister made more sense than he gave her credit for. What else did he have to lose? He already hadn't slept all night since she left the ranch. Every morning he left early enough to make it into town and drive by her house while she was still asleep. He told himself it was just to check on things to do with the house before he went on to the coffee shop, but that was a crock. He was close to her. Seeing her on the street in front of the post office was a knife in the gut. She looked so beautiful and it rubbed salt in the wounds.

She was getting on with her life and he was glad for her.

But he felt she was further away from him than before. Thomas had to accept his first wife turning her back on him and their child. In truth, it hadn't touched his heart. He had to come to terms with that fact. But he had to realize that Jamie Westmoreland had taken his heart and walked away with it when she left. Tori was right. Jamie deserved to hear the words wide awake. And it had to mean something special, maybe something that would convince her to give him a chance. Maybe she could love him back. He just had to give it some thought.

AFTER TWO DAYS, Jamie had debated with herself over and over, and finally talked herself into picking up the phone and calling the ranch. She reached for the phone on the table beside her just as it rang at the same time. When she saw the caller ID, her heart began to race in earnest. It was Thomas.

Jamie took in a calming breath. "Hello."

"Hi, this is Thomas. I didn't catch you at a bad time, did I?"

"No, this is fine. This is my weekend off."

"That's good." There was a couple of moments of silence.

"How is Andy? And everyone at the ranch?"

"They're all fine. In fact, Andy is the reason I'm calling. It's a perfect day for a swim, but Andy asked to go to the swimming hole instead of the pool. And we'll take along some food and make an afternoon of it. You remember the swimming hole I told you about, right?"

"Yes, I remember you said it was your family's best-kept secret. It sounds like a good way to spend such a warm afternoon."

"Andy and I hope you'll want to come along. It'll be relaxing and Andy's been asking several times a day about you and when he can see you again."

The ball was in her court. He waited. Andy wanted to see her. She wanted to see the little boy. And Pops and Dottie and all the rest. But also she needed to see Thomas. He had just said he wanted her to come along. She was done being timid or hesitant in her life.

"I think that is the best invitation I've ever received. I'll get my things together and be there within the hour?"

She smiled as she noted the mixture of relief and pleased surprise in his tones. "That sounds good. We'll be packed up and waiting. You just made a couple of cowboys happy. See you soon."

Her reflection caught her eye across the room, beaming back at her from the mirror over the couch. Her own grin of happiness at the prospect combined with his words and it couldn't get much wider. She quickly moved to the closet in her bedroom and began selecting a swimsuit and cover-up, appropriate footwear for the rocky path she remembered. Then she decided to change into her two-piece suit with its swirls of bright fuchsia and neon blues on a black background. It fit her curves very nicely and was sexy but not too much so…after all, they would be chaperoned by a seven-year-old on this visit to the swimming hole. A pair of cut-off denim jeans and a bright blue sleeveless top would do. Her cover-up, a large beach towel, sun visor, lotion, and a pair of swim shoes went into her beach bag. She piled her hair on top of her head and secured it with a couple of combs. She grabbed her sunglasses and small purse with her car keys as she headed out the door.

Her feet fairly flew along the sidewalk to the car. The smile had not left her face since the phone call, and as the car ate up the miles from town to the ranch's gates, she had to mind the fact she was pushing the speed limit in her barely contained nervous excitement. At the same time, she tried to remind herself that this was just an invitation to go swimming on a hot day. Then she pushed away the cautionary small voice and shook it out of her mind. Nothing was going to dampen her spirits. She was going to enjoy the moments that came her way.

"She's here! Nurse Jamie's here! Hurry, Dad!" The screen door slammed behind Andy just after Jasper scooted through it. The small figure came flying as a bullet straight and true down the steps and along the sidewalk and ended up in a halt as Jamie shut off the engine and opened her door. She had barely cleared the car door when two arms caught her in a bear hug around her waist and Jasper chimed in with excited barks.

She's here…finally. He might not have shouted the words aloud as his son had done, but Thomas's brain was repeating them as he crossed the porch and came down the steps, his gaze shielded by the dark lens of his sunshades. They allowed him to soak up the beautiful vision of the woman, her arms embracing Andy, her head thrown back in lighthearted laughter. His whole body was alive at the sight of her. And when she turned those doe eyes upon him over Andy's head, the jolt of electricity went straight into his heart and zipped along each and every nerve ending. It was taking every ounce of control not to allow himself to follow the lead of his son and sweep the woman up and off her feet into his arms and never let her go again. He increased his grips on the bag in one hand and the picnic basket in the other.

"I hope I'm not running too late?"

He shook his head, as he placed the bag and basket over the tailgate of his pickup and then turned to reach for the bag she held. She handed it over to him. "You're right on time."

"Let's go, Dad. I can hardly wait to show Nurse Jamie our swimming place." Andy had taken possession of Jamie's hand and was leading her toward the front of the truck. She held the door open to the back seat for him to climb in, and

Jasper followed with a swift jump on his own. She turned and found her door was open and Thomas stood next to it. She might get used to having her door opened by a certain cowboy on a regular basis. She stepped onto the running board and then slid into the passenger seat.

Thomas took his place and they headed off down the driveway. "How come we couldn't ride our horses to the swimming hole today, Dad?"

"This is faster, and we have our swimming things and food to take along today. We'll do that next time."

"And then you can ride Mischief Maker again, Nurse Jamie." Andy was planning it all out in his mind.

"I think since I'm not here anymore in my nursing capacity, it might be okay for you just to call me Jamie. How does that sound?" She smiled at the little boy over her shoulder and was rewarded with a huge grin.

"That's cool."

"And that goes for me, too?" Thomas turned his head and gave a smile. She took a moment to consider the question. He noted that she seemed to enjoy teasing him a bit, and then she relented with a nod.

"I think you may do the same."

Andy had to catch her up on all the news of the end of the school term. Thomas couldn't help but notice the change in Andy since he had told him that Jamie had accepted their invitation earlier that day. Right now, he was more animated than he had seen him in the last four weeks. And it was all because of Jamie. She came, she saw, she conquered both his heart and his son's. He had to wonder if she had any idea of the impact she had made in their lives. He needed to have time to talk to her today. Tori had said Jamie was in love with him. But what did she really know about the subject? Look how long she had kept Gray Dalton guessing on the subject? He needed to explore that subject for himself.

"Here we are, Jamie! The water is really cold when you first get in, so it's best to just jump in. Right, Dad? But Dad and me and Aunt Tori and my uncles…we all swing off the rope swing."

"Well, we'll let Jamie decide the way she wants to do it for her first time here. You and Jasper run ahead and pick out a spot for the blanket and picnic basket. No getting into the water until I'm there. Okay?"

"Yes, sir. Got it." He and the dog scrambled out of the truck and took off down the path. Jamie met Thomas at the back of the truck. He handed her the blanket and her bag. She reached in and picked up the other bag, as well.

"I can carry the bags and you've got the picnic basket and the cooler."

"I know better than to not go along with your instructions…whether you're in scrubs and on duty or not. Lead on."

When they reached the banks of the swimming hole, they found that Andy had chosen a very good spot between two tall cypress trees, elevated a bit along the riverbank.

There was a smattering of soft green grass for the blanket to be spread upon.

"This is a great spot, Andy. And the water is so incredibly blue and clear along this bank. How deep is it, do you think?" She set the bags down as Thomas finished spreading out the blanket.

"It's about two to five feet along this side. Then out past that, where it gets darker blue, you'll have anywhere from six to eighteen feet. That's where we have the rope swing."

"That tree is huge," Jamie said, looking to the long length of knotted rope and the massive branches that supported the swing. Farther over, the river was creating a few feet of rapids as the current swept over the limestone bottom and smaller boulders that created the soft rushing sound of water that helped break up the stillness of the spot. They could have been the only humans on the planet, the area was so isolated.

Andy had made quick work of shedding his clothing down to the cut-off jean shorts he wore as swim trunks. He reached into their swim bag and came out with a bottle of lotion.

"Can you help me, Jamie?" He held the bottle out to her. She smiled and went to work, just as if the two of them had been doing something that simple for ages.

Thomas watched the pair. His mind and heart were already of one accord. He needed to know if Jamie felt the same.

"Hurry up, Dad," Andy said, bringing Thomas back to the present moment. "We need to show Jamie how we jump in from the rope swing."

"Okay." Thomas grinned. "I'm right behind you. Meet you over on the steps." Andy thanked Jamie and took off around the riverbank.

Jamie stood and began removing her shorts and top. Thomas tried not to stare, but it was taking all his willpower. The swimsuit wasn't exactly a bikini, but it showed off all her best assets. Thomas knew he needed to get in the cold water as fast as he could, but he needed to try to be a gentleman and offer to help with the lotion she was smoothing on the skin of her shoulders and arms. "Need help with your back?"

You are a glutton for punishment, Tremayne. When she handed him the bottle with a smile and turned to give him access to her back, he was digging deep for that willpower.

"It's a pain having fair skin," she was saying. "I always envied people who had natural tans. I turn red and then just tan a very little."

Thomas tried to concentrate on her words. But the smooth, soft skin beneath his palms was becoming addicting. He could spend hours smoothing lotion over her entire body, and he'd offer to do so...except there was a third member of their little group. He flipped the bottle top shut and handed it back to her. "All done."

She looked a bit flushed and not able to make full eye

contact with him. Was it the heat of the afternoon or was she feeling something along the same lines he was at the moment? *Interesting.*

"Are you going to wade in from here?"

She met his gaze with a determined smile on her face. "You two males think I'm some timid female and wouldn't want to do the rope swing, too? I'm game to try something new."

He grabbed her hand and met her smile. "Then let's see what you've got, pretty lady."

WHAT ARE YOU doing? Why had she said she wanted to go off the rope swing? Standing beside the tree and looking upward…Jamie might as well have been looking up at a four-story building. That's what it seemed like from her vantage spot. Of course, she had also said the first thing that had come into her mind as Thomas had finished smoothing his hands over her body. She had stood as still as possible and tried to not show it was having any effect on her. It had a major effect on her, and she had needed to break the tension that was building inside her. When he asked the question, she said the first thing that came to mind. This would teach her.

"Watch me, Jamie," Andy called from the small platform way above their heads.

"I'm watching, Andy. You be careful up there, okay?"

"No problem! And Dad's a really good teacher so he'll show you what to do."

"Andy's been doing this since he was five. He began on the lower rope we had in place at first. Then one day, he just climbed right up and off he went. Don't worry. He wouldn't be up there if I didn't know he could do it safely." Thomas's words were meant to quiet any misgivings she had for the child. Now, if his words could do the same for her nerves and worry over her own performance that was about to happen, she'd be in better shape.

Andy pushed off from the platform and swung in a wide arc out over the water, then gave a loud "whoop" and let go of the rope. The splash was a good one, and in seconds, Andy's head bobbed to the surface and he raised a hand with a thumbs-up. "Come on in, you guys."

"Okay…I'll go up first and you place your hands and feet where I put mine as you follow. It's as easy as climbing any ladder." Thomas looked at her as he spoke to make certain she would be okay. She nodded.

"No problem."

She kept reminding herself that she had said those words as she began the climb, following every move that Thomas made until they stood side by side on the platform high above the water. There wasn't a lot of room on the boards and she and Thomas were in very close quarters.

"It's up to you. Do you want to go next, or do you want

me to go?"

"Which do you think?" She wanted his advice.

"I think you should go so I can help give you an extra push so you can gain some good height before you release. You'll hold on...both hands laced just above the knot. You'll swing out and use your legs like you would on a regular swing and when you come back toward me, I'll give you another good push and when you reach the highest point in your swing, just let go and be prepared for a little shock when you hit the water. It's cold spring-fed water so it can give a jolt on a hot day. Got it all?"

She nodded. "I've got it."

Thomas's gaze centered on hers. "You don't have to do this if you would rather wait."

She met his gaze head-on. "I know that. But it's something I want to do. I'm not backing down or sitting on the sidelines."

Thomas didn't ask for clarification. He nodded. "Then grab on tight, and I'll give you a push."

Jamie held on and things happened quickly. Before she knew it, she felt herself falling through the air and then the water swallowed her, and her breath was sucked out of her by the absolute freezing temperature of the water. She didn't wait to touch bottom. Jamie began her climb back to the surface and when she broke the surface, both Andy and Thomas were yelling their approval and clapping. She swam toward the shore and the natural stone steps that would get her back onto land. Pushing the wet hair out of her eyes, she looked upward. Thomas hit the water next. By the time he made it to the edge, she was on her way up the tree ladder again. For the next half hour, the trio swam, took turns on the rope swing, and generally had an amazing time in the water.

Andy was the one to remind them that they had brought food. It was time to dry off and hit the picnic basket of goodies. There was cold fried chicken, fresh sliced watermelon, potato salad, chips, and cookies.

"I helped Dad put the food together," Andy volunteered as he took the plate from Jamie. "I remembered you said you liked your chicken cold and not hot."

"Thank you, Andy. I appreciate you remembered that. Everything you and your dad chose is very good. Either that or I really worked up an appetite during all that swimming."

"My uncle Trey and me have a watermelon seed spitting contest whenever we eat watermelon. Do you know how to do that?"

Jamie examined her slice for seeds. "You go first and let's see if I can beat you."

Her first couple of tries failed miserably, but she didn't give up. Andy won the first go-around. But she powered back to take the second one by a mere inch. Andy managed to win the third one.

After that bit of fun, Andy stood up and announced that he and Jasper were going to go along the shallows in search of minnows for his fishing pole. Thomas told him where the boundaries were, and he needed to see the top of his head where his favorite fishing site was. He and Jasper headed off.

"More food?" Thomas offered her the last remaining cookie.

She held up her hand and shook her head. "Not another bite. It was all very good, but I'm stuffed. Thank you for doing all of this and inviting me to come along. I haven't had so much fun and felt so relaxed in a very, very long time."

Thomas nodded, putting the last of the containers into the basket and setting it aside. He stretched out his long legs and propped himself on his elbow, close to where she was in much the same position. The peace of the late afternoon settled around them, the sound of the rushing water a lulling comfort.

"I think this just might be a little piece of heaven on earth right here in this spot. Thanks again for having this idea."

"I'm beginning to agree with you. But for me, it has a lot to do with the company involved. I hope you know that you have really elevated the bar today where you're concerned in Andy's estimation. Not only are you a female who doesn't shy away from holding lizards and frogs, but you can spit a pretty good distance and climb a huge tree and swing from a rope without blinking an eye. You set the bar high there."

Jamie basked in the dappled sunlight playing over them

and its warmth, but the real warmth she felt came across to her from a pair of deep blue eyes that she knew she had already succumbed to drowning in their depths…forget the river in front of them. "I hope you know that you raised an amazing little boy. I've missed him. And everyone else who made me feel so at ease and welcomed from that first day I came out here to take care of a problem patient." She grinned across the space.

"I apologize for being that problem patient. It was a lucky day for all of us when I got hurt and landed in that hospital bed. How else would our paths have crossed? I'm glad I could take one for the team."

His hand brushed a few errant strands of hair that fell across her shoulder in the growing breeze. She didn't flinch away as a finger remained, lazily tracing a pattern on the bare shoulder. Thomas's gaze darkened as it stayed in command of hers. "I missed you, Jamie. But I can see the change in you. You seem freer, more at ease in your own skin. That's the best way I can put it."

"That is a good way to put it. The time with the counselor and dealing with shadows from the past that I didn't even realize were still with me… It's hard to explain. But they're gone and I was able to discover strengths I didn't realize I have. I was able to do that because of the support of so many friends here in Faris…at the hospital, in town, and here on this ranch. I knew you supported me even while you might not have understood why I kept you away these last few weeks. I'm grateful that you didn't just say forget it and walk away."

"I hate to tell you this, Jamie Westmoreland," he began, his words low, a definitive set to his jawline. His two fingers slid downward, slowly, tantalizing with the heated trail they left until they found the valley of the deep vee of her swimsuit top and came to rest. Jamie's breath was harder to draw inward, but she was locked in a cobalt-blue spell of his gaze that drew closer as the pressure increased via fingers that drew her toward the flame that waited with his lips. "Walking away from something I want so badly has never been an option." His breath was warm against her cheek and then there was no space between them. His mouth claimed hers and they were more than ready to welcome him.

Jamie was in the one place she had longed to be and had doubted she would be again. It was the feeling of fully coming home…and coming alive all wrapped in one explosion of feeling. The weight of his body pushed against hers and her back felt the blanket welcome her as his body fitted his length against hers. Her palms relished the feel of gliding over strong shoulders, their flesh heated by the sun and that heat filtering throughout her body. His mouth moved along her jaw to draw a soft moan from her as his teeth lightly tugged on the earlobe. Then an explosion of heat filled her inner core as those two fingers that drew her to him earlier, slid along the fabric and over the crest of one breast, seeking and finding the contact they sought with a very hard and aching nipple. He reacted to her swift intake of breath, his mouth drawing in the throbbing nub and sending sparks of light beneath closed eyes as her body arched itself toward the pleasurable sensation.

"Dad...Dad, come quick! I got a fish, Dad. Hurry!" The voice was shrill in the silence and filtered through both their brains at the same time.

A muttered oath escaped the mouth of the man who moved the cloth back into place and then allowed his lips to rest against her throat. "Are you serious? If I don't go, he'll drag the fish over here or end up in the river with it."

Jamie was both disappointed and yet saw humor in the situation. She shook her head. "You better go."

Thomas raised up to allow his gaze to take in her face. A slow smile softened the look into a tenderness that Jamie had never imagined anyone would ever look at her with. It plunged straight to her heart. "This conversation will be continued later...in a much more secluded and comfortable place. Remember that." Then he placed a swift kiss on her lips and in one move, he grabbed a beach towel and stood, wrapping the towel around the waist of his swim trunks. He flashed a grin at her and strode away. Her cheeks had the good graces to heat up as she realized he was concealing evidence of just how involved his body was with their earlier "conversation." She stifled a soft giggle. The world was right with itself and the possibilities abounded in the warmth of sunlight and laughter of a child and his dad's deeper tones in the distance. Jamie whispered a prayer in her heart. *Could this be forever?*

Chapter Eighteen

THREE DAYS HAD passed. Three days since the picnic at the swimming hole. She had only had three texts from the man. And they were brief. She knew from a conversation with Dottie at the supermarket the previous evening, that new stock had to be moved due to a lightning fire in one of their far-flung pastures. It kept them all on their toes for a couple of days. Jamie tried to understand the factors involved with all of that. But still…she wanted to hear Thomas's voice.

On the morning of the fourth day, she decided to take matters into her own hands. She picked up the phone, intent on inviting herself out to the ranch. If the mountain wouldn't or couldn't come to her…then she would just go to it. On the third ring, she had readied herself to hopefully hear Thomas's voice on the other end. Her plan went awry.

"Hey, girl," Tori replied, when she recognized Jamie's voice. "This is a surprise."

"I guess it is. I thought you might be on the road. I was just calling to invite myself out to go riding with Andy. Both Thomas and Andy said it would be a good idea, and I have some time today before I go to work and…"

"Oh…wow. Today?"

Tori's tepid response caught her off guard. "Well, I thought today, but if tomorrow would be better if he has other plans or…"

"Yes, that's right. He *does*. In fact, he and his dad went camping. They'll be back in a couple of days. But you have to work today, correct?"

"Yes, I'm evaluating a new hire on the evening shift."

"I see. So you will be at work after three today."

Jamie couldn't put her finger on it, but Tori sounded a bit strange…even for Tori. Maybe she had called at the wrong time? Maybe it was all a bad idea on her part. "Look, let's just take a rain check on the ride. I'll call again and we can plan something when people have more time. It's no big deal. I'm glad he and his dad are doing something fun together."

"That's sounds like a better idea." Tori almost sounded relieved. "Give us a call in a few days. I've got to run right now. But you have a good evening at work. I'm sure we'll see each other before I leave again. Bye!"

Jamie responded "bye" to an already empty line. It was all very odd, but there was nothing more to do. Funny that Dottie hadn't mentioned the camping trip, just the fire. Maybe Thomas felt he needed to do something to take Andy's mind off of it or something along those lines? She pushed the disappointment she felt down and began getting ready to go on to the hospital. Her frame of mind wasn't great, but she'd hope that work would distract her.

An hour into the shift, things were very quiet. Jamie had given the new nurse some orders to chart and she was at the computer in the conference room working on them. Jamie was seated at the front desk, trying to keep her brain concentrating on the screen in front of her. The other nurses were off down the hall, presumably busy with the half dozen patients on the surgical floor. Then she heard a small voice.

"S'cuse me." Was it déjà vu? Was she hearing things? "S'cuse me, please? I'm down here again." Jamie scooted her chair back, rising to look over the counter. She saw the familiar black cowboy hat and then the blue eyes that had first captured her heart.

"Andy, whatever are you doing here? Is someone in the hospital? Is it your dad? Pops?" Her heart pushed to her throat, hoping against hope that his dad hadn't met with another accident. "How did you get here?"

"No one's in the hospital 'cept you. And we came to talk to you. We need to ask a question."

"We? Who is *we*?"

"That would be him and me."

She jerked her gaze from the child and saw Thomas standing a few feet away. He looked so good standing there in black jeans, a crisp white shirt, and a dark navy western-cut jacket, black boots, and his black Stetson. She would never tire of looking at the man. Her pulse was pounding in her ears. Andy moved to stand next to his dad, and Jamie couldn't contain the smile any longer. Andy was dressed almost identically to his dad. And they stood side by side with the same stance, one hand behind their backs. Whatever was going on?

"I thought you were camping?" She said the first thing that she found words for.

"That was Tori's hastily concocted excuse."

"Jasper came, too. We had to get real special permission for him to come see you," Andy spoke up again. The dog came from around the corner right on cue. He even had a navy bandanna tied around his neck.

"Special permission?" Jamie asked. She was still trying to grasp why they were there. What was going on? And who let a dog in? He wasn't one of the therapy animals that were allowed to visit patients once a week.

"Dr. Cuesta gave the okay," Thomas spoke up. "Jasper promised to be on his best behavior. We thought about doing this at your house, but then we decided this would be more appropriate because it's where the *both* of us first met you. So, here we are."

Doing this… Whatever were they up to?

Thomas nodded at his son. Andy cleared his throat and stepped forward. "You need to come in front of the desk thing." And then he remembered. "*Please.* Please come in front of the desk thing."

Jamie stifled a grin but did as he directed. She stopped in

front of him. Then he motioned with his free hand. "You need to do what you did then. You bent down to talk to me. Remember?"

"I remember." She settled on her ankles so she was on his eye level.

He glanced up at his dad and Thomas nodded. Andy took a deep breath and began.

"I think you're a real cool lady. And real pretty, too. You're a good nurse and you take good care of people. You're really brave, too. And you like Jasper, and you'll be a good rider with a lot more practice, but I can help you. And I like it when I come downstairs and you're cooking blueberry pancakes just like I like." Jamie couldn't contain the smile any longer. He was trying to be such a little grown-up…just like the first day they met. "My dad and I had a long talk, and I wanted to tell you all this because I think you'd make a real good mom, too. And I could be a good son. I'd *really* try to be. And I'd really like it if you could like my dad a lot, too. I brought you these. I picked them out myself."

The hand behind his back had been concealing a mixture of pink and yellow and purple and green flowers. A few that might be classified as weeds, but he had clearly chosen them and might have picked them, too. The ribbon he had tied around the stalks resembled a strip of canvas. He presented it to her with such solemn regard. Jamie knew that it was the most beautiful bouquet she could ever hope to receive. His words had brought tears to her eyes, and she tried to blink them away. He stepped back next to his dad.

"Okay, Dad, it's your turn. And she's already crying so you might want to get her a tissue thing. She might like that."

"Thanks, son, I think I've got it now." Thomas held out his hand to help her stand up. He let go of her hand and reached into his pocket. He had come prepared with a crisp, white handkerchief. Thomas handed it to her. She took it, taking in a deep breath, her heart pounding out of her chest. The look in his eyes carried the warmth of sunshine, and it was shining on her.

"I thought for many years that my son and I had each other and that was all we needed...to be a family and all. But I was wrong. I realized that when I woke up in this hospital and looked into a pair of eyes that I have carried with me every moment of my days since then. They were gentle and cautious and held a warmth I had not known before. I fought the idea, though. I admit it.

"I did because I was afraid. What if you couldn't care about us? What if I made a mistake? But I was soon proven wrong. You won over every person who met you while at the ranch. You didn't stand back...you simply fit right in. You took such care of Andy and had such patience with him. You gave my sass right back to me as good as I dished it out. Then one day it hit me like a two-by-four. I couldn't remember what it was like before you came into our lives. And I couldn't imagine what it would be like without you there going forward each day. I've never been good with the words that I'm told women like to hear, but I also brought these."

The bouquet he was holding was all red roses and a red satin bow; streamers held them together. "In case you didn't hear me the first time I spoke these words, let me make it very clear now." He drew her close using the hand he had captured again. He laid her palm on the center of his chest, over his heart. "My heart beats faster because of you. I love you, Jamie Westmoreland. Yesterday, today, and all the tomorrows I hope we can share together. That will never change as long as I live and breathe. Andy chose you and so do I. The question is, could you love us and choose us, too?"

"Daaad...geez, you forgot." The words came from Andy in a loud whisper tinged with exasperation. He nodded his head and Thomas got the message.

"Thanks, son. Just when I thought I was doing pretty good. Let's back up." He looked at Jamie with such apology in his eyes. He made a movement, and Jasper came trotting up to stand between them. He barked once.

"That's Jasper saying he agrees that you need to be part of our family. He voted for you, too." Andy clarified the "dog-speak."

Thomas had bent over and was moving the material of the bandanna around the dog's neck. When he straightened, there was a small jeweler's box in his palm. Andy's hand jerked on the hem of his jacket. Thomas looked down at him. Andy pointed to the floor. Thomas took a deep breath and then went down on one knee.

"I wanted this to be perfect for you. But I hope you know that we did all of this because you deserve it and so much more. Will you marry us, Jamie?"

Jamie had given up on trying to keep the tears locked away. All she could do was wipe them away as soon as they began to run down her cheeks. Everything that she had ever dreamed of was in front of her. Her heart was full and overflowing, and the words were in her brain, but all she could do was nod her head. The ring slipped onto her finger. Finally, the words came out. "I think this is the most perfect proposal any woman ever had. And I will cherish it all the days of my life. Because I happen to love each of you, too. And I can't think of anything better than to be your mother, Andy…and your wife, Thomas."

Andy let out a loud whoop and wrapped his arms around her waist. "She said yes!"

Thomas stood up and their lips met in a sweet promise. Jasper added his two cents. When she could catch her breath, she realized that Dr. Cuesta and the rest of the staff on the floor had appeared from other rooms to offer congratulations and join in the happy moment. They had just been waiting for Andy's shout. And they were joined by Truitt and Trey, and Tori with tears streaming down her cheeks. Gray stood with his arm about her shoulders grinning from ear to ear. And Pops and Dottie weren't to be left out.

Thomas grinned, his arm drawing her against his side.

"Get used to being the center of this family…and with lots of friends who love you, too."

Jamie buried her face in the profusion of blooms in her arms. Never could she have imagined such love surrounding her in her lifetime. Filled with so much joy, she looked up and met Thomas's blue gaze. It held every promise of every dream she had prayed for, plus more. Three hearts had become one.

Chapter Nineteen

"WHY CAN'T I go on the honeymoon? If this is a family, I should get a vote, too." Andy was not pleased by the turn of events that had been brought to his attention a couple of days before the wedding. He tried once more to get his point across even as his uncle Trey was adjusting the bolo tie that he was being made to wear in order to match the other males in the wedding party.

"Sorry, buddy. A honeymoon is meant for two people only. Three is definitely a crowd. But you get to hang out with me and Truitt and Tori. A couple of the rodeos have huge carnivals, and that means there will be lots of rides and lots of junk food. You and I will make ourselves sick and have fun doing it."

Andy gave it some consideration. "I don't really like sand. And what's there to do on an island but fish? I guess it'd be more fun going to a carnival and rodeo. I don't get why Dad and my new mom don't want to come with us instead."

Trey grinned as he finished up the tie. "One of these days, I'll remind you of this conversation. When you're getting married."

"No way, yuk. I don't like girls. They're too fussy."

"Really? So I'm hearing you don't like your favorite aunt? And what about Jamie?" Tori had stepped into the room and caught the last of the conversation.

Andy gave a deep sigh. "Okay. You're not a real girl…you know, like the others. You're Tori and you like doing fun stuff. You have bulls as pets and that's not a girl thing. And Jamie…well she's cool and all and she's my mom. But other girls are just…just…"

Trey nodded. "I got it, buddy. I totally understand and agree. And you hang on to that belief as long as you possibly can. Now, get a move on so we can get to the cake and food part of this day."

Tori checked in on Truitt next, who was keeping his eyes on both the nervous groom and the ring bearer. "Are you sure that the rings won't be rolling down the aisle at any point in this ceremony? Because if they do, I will…"

"They won't," Truitt said back to her in a mock whisper that matched hers. "It's called the magic of Velcro. And Andy has worked with that dog for hours a day on his job. Just relax. All that matters is that the bride and groom say, 'I do' and the preacher pronounces them married. The rest is just a lot of…"

Tori held up her hand to stop him. "*Please* keep your typical male response to yourself. And why is Thomas standing out there at the fence staring into an empty corral? He'll have dust on his boots I personally just had shined." Truitt stood up from the rocking chair he had been keeping vigil from on the side porch. "We'll all be in our places with bright, shiny faces. Isn't that how the saying goes?"

Tori shook her head and shot him a look of exasperation as she left him. "If we were still in kindergarten."

Truitt walked down to the corral and took up much the same stance as his brother...one boot hooked over the bottom rung, arms resting on the top rail. Neither spoke for a few moments.

"Second thoughts?" Truitt decided to be his usual direct self.

"No way." Thomas was succinct in his response. "Maybe a bit nervous. You remember my first trip down the matrimonial aisle didn't end up so well. And I don't want to ever put any of us through that again."

"You and Jamie were meant to be. The other was just a measuring stick for you. When the real thing came along, you knew it."

Neither of them had ventured a look at each other, but it was an important conversation all the more for both of them. Thomas clasped his hands together as he leaned on the railing. "It's days like today that I miss Mom and Dad even more. I think about our little brother. And I think about your Skyler. I know it might not be easy for you standing up there today at the altar and all. I'd understand if you didn't want to do it."

"I laid Skyler to rest a while ago. It wasn't right to try and keep her alive and here with me…if you know what I mean. I buried her in the wedding dress she never got to wear on the wedding day we never got to have. You can't live in the past…or so I've been told often enough. My advice to you on this day: Hold on to Jamie's hand as tight as you can and be grateful each morning when you wake up and see her face on the pillow beside yours. Don't waste a minute.

"And since we've just a few minutes to go before this big day takes off…I may not have said the words out loud before. But I'm damn glad you survived that day. And that you had the strength to hold the rest of us together. That's why the three of us are happy that you found Jamie and Andy has the mom he wanted. Because you deserve this new life you begin today, because you walked the tough road to get here…and you brought the rest of us along with you. So there's that. And now, according to our sister, you are to get your butt inside and dust off those boots again."

Truitt turned back toward the house. Thomas said his silent goodbyes to those he carried with him daily. However, he had a strange feeling that his mom would find a way to keep her eye on all of them today. And he had a bride waiting on him. *His Jamie.*

"SOMETHING OLD, SOMETHING new, something blue...and something borrowed." Tori stepped forward and handed over the gold cross with the thin gold chain. "It was our mom's. I know she had wanted to give it to Skyler when she and Truitt got married. She thought it would be nice to start a tradition with the brides that came along in the family. She was sentimental like that." Tori took a moment to blink something out of her eye. "Who knows...it might be nice. And I know she'd want you to wear it now. If you want to or..."

Jamie took the necklace from her. "I think it is *perfect* to begin this tradition today. A Tremayne tradition. I will be proud to be the one today. And I am beyond proud to be joining your family. It'll be my first real one...a family. I just hope I can live up to it."

Tori shared a hug with her, careful to not mess up the folds of satin and lace. Jamie was gorgeous, and Thomas would be blown away when his bride started down the aisle. Tori stepped back and helped to adjust the veil after the slender necklace was fastened around Jamie's neck.

Jamie checked her reflection once more in the mirror. She had fallen in love with the second dress she had tried on. It was slender fitting until it flared a bit from the knees down to the floor. A shimmer of satin overlaid with white lace. The three-quarter-length sleeves were lace only. The squared neckline showed off the small cross perfectly. The long length of tulle veil was caught and fastened at the back of her updo. A bouquet of red roses and white stephanotis was ready for her walk down the aisle that had been transformed from the front steps of the house across the garden where chairs sat for the sixty or so ceremony guests. Later in the evening, there would be a dinner reception for another hundred plus guests invited to join in those celebrations.

The bride's music began, and Jamie walked out onto the porch. For a moment, she flashed back to the first time she drove up to the house and came up those steps to stand where she was right now. She had been so ambivalent, a little nervous, and a whole lot determined to leave as soon as possible. She smiled at how that attitude had changed. Now she never wanted to leave what she considered to be the most beautiful place on earth. A place she would forever call home. Pops waited at the bottom of the steps for her. He looked very handsome, with his usual scruffy face trimmed up and the new black suit and hat fitted to a fidgeting body of nerves.

Jamie took careful steps down to stand beside him, her hand gently curving around his arm. She gave him a bright smile. "Thanks for doing this today, Pops. It means a lot."

"Well, I never had any daughter of my own to take down an aisle or whatever. Didn't think it was in my cards. But looks like I was wrong. And it's a real great honor to do it today for you and Thomas. I just hope I get it all done the right way."

Jamie heard the slight tremor in his voice, and she even spied a bit of moisture before he blinked it away from the corner of his eye. He was a dear man, and she treasured the fact he had taken her under his wing the last couple of months. Before long, she had even managed to saddle her own horse and earned his praise as a budding horsewoman. He was an added blessing in her life…right along with Dottie, and all the rest of the Tremayne family and the ranch hands and their families.

She wasn't alone any longer, only able to depend upon herself. She was part of a group of people who didn't stifle anyone's independence but were there for backup whenever needed and to be cheerleaders and provide a safe place to catch one's breath for the next day. She finally knew what it felt like to take a deep breath of fresh air and allow it to escape with a smile. Andy and Thomas brought only smiles to her heart, and she couldn't remember what her life was before them.

The shadows had evaporated. Today, the glorious Texas sun was shining in a bluebonnet-blue sky above. Jamie held back the urge to run down the aisle to grab hold of her new life. Instead, she strolled along on Pops's arm, her gaze joining Thomas's. Then she simply glided on happiness.

THOMAS SPOKE HIS vows in sure tones. Andy stood next to

him, nodding his approval. Truitt and Trey did their part under Tori's watchful eye from her place next to the bride. Dottie kept her lacy hanky dabbing eyes throughout the ceremony. And Jasper had performed his duty of walking down the aisle and standing quietly while Truitt untied the rings and handed them over to the pastor. Then Jasper sat beside Pops in the front row.

When Thomas watched Jamie walk up the aisle toward him earlier, he thought he would either pass out or run and scoop her up against him and never let her go. It was more apparent to him each day and even more so on his wedding day, that for the first time, he finally knew what love was all about. Smiling was a very good thing. His life was complete…with Jamie and Andy.

There had even been a moment during the wedding prayer that a sweet bit of breeze had made him look up and on the branch behind the pastor sat a bright red cardinal, watching over the festivities. It wasn't really the season for them. But this one seemed not to note that fact. Thomas smiled as his heart filled to capacity. His mom had always said that a cardinal appeared to bring love from someone in Heaven.

His hand closed securely around Jamie's as it rested in his palm. His gaze went to meet the one that waited for his. Jamie's smile would forever be his renewed strength and hope in the future. Then his eyes raised once more to the branch where the bright red bird still sat in silence, observing the pair. His smile came from deep within. Jamie had been the sweet gift his heart had been waiting for. Thomas whispered on the soft breeze… *Thanks, Mom.*

The End

Want more? Check out Debra Holt's *True Blue Cowboy*!

Join Tule Publishing's newsletter for more great reads and weekly deals!

If you enjoyed *Capturing the Texas Rancher's Heart,* you'll love the next book in….

The Tremaynes of Texas series

Book 1: *Capturing the Texas Rancher's Heart*

Book 2: *The Rancher Risks It All*
Coming July 2021!

Available now at your favorite online retailer!

More books by Debra Holt

The Blood Brothers series

Book 1: *True Blue Cowboy*

Book 2: *Homeward Bound, Cowboy*

Book 3: *Her Secret Cowboy*

The Texas Lawmen series

Book 1: *Beware the Ranger*

Book 2: *The Lawman's Apache Moon*

Book 3: *Along Came a Ranger*

Book 4: *The Sheriff's Christmas Angels*

Available now at your favorite online retailer!

About the Author

Born and raised in the Lone Star state of Texas, Debra grew up among horses, cowboys, wide open spaces, and real Texas Rangers. Pride in her state and ancestry knows no bounds and it is these heroes and heroines she loves to write about the most. She also draws upon a variety of life experiences including working with abused children, caring for baby animals at a major zoo, and planning high-end weddings (ah, romance!).

Debra's real pride and joys, however, are her son, an aspiring film actor, and a daughter with aspirations to join the Federal Bureau of Investigation (more story ideas!). When she isn't busy writing about tall Texans and feisty heroines, she can be found cheering on her Texas Tech Red Raiders, or heading off on another cruise adventure. She read her first romance, Janet Dailey's *Fiesta San Antonio*, over thirty years ago and became hooked on the genre. Writing contemporary western romance is both her passion and dream come true, and she hopes her books will bring smiles…and sighs…to all who believe in happily-ever-after's.

Thank you for reading

Capturing the Texas Rancher's Heart

If you enjoyed this book, you can find more from all our great authors at TulePublishing.com, or from your favorite online retailer.

Made in United States
North Haven, CT
22 November 2021